FRIEND
OF ACPL

FROM THE
LIGHTHOUSE

FROM THE LIGHTHOUSE

Liz Chipman

DUTTON CHILDREN'S BOOKS

NEW YORK

The excerpt on page 125 is from *A Hudson Riverbook*, by William F. Gekle, copyright © 1978 by William F. Gekle. Used by permission.

On page vii, "The Lordly Hudson," by Paul Goodman, copyright © 1962 by Paul Goodman. Copyright renewed 1990 by Sally Goodman. Used by permission.

Library of Congress Cataloging-in-Publication Data

Chipman, Liz.
From the lighthouse / by Liz Chipman.—1st ed.
p. cm.
Summary: In 1938, thirteen-year-old Louise Bloom tries to figure out what caused her mother to leave her, her three brothers, their father, and the lighthouse on the Hudson River that they call home.
ISBN: 0-525-47312-2
[1. Mothers—Fiction. 2. Single-parent families—Fiction. 3. Family problems—Fiction. 4. Lighthouses—Fiction. 5. Hudson River Valley (N.Y. and N.J.)—Fiction. 6. New York (State)—History—20th century—Fiction.] I. Title.
PZ7.C4435Fr 2004
[Fic]—dc22   2003023634

Published in the United States by Dutton Children's Books,
a division of Penguin Young Readers Group
345 Hudson Street, New York, New York 10014
www.penguin.com

Designed by Irene Vandervoort

Printed in USA   First Edition
1 3 5 7 9 10 8 6 4 2

For my grandmother,
Eva Sandstrom Masterman

━━━
━━━

And my mother,
Janis Masterman Bennett

"Driver, what stream is it?" I asked, well knowing
it was our lordly Hudson hardly flowing,
"It is our lordly Hudson hardly flowing,"
he said, "under the green-grown cliffs."

Be still, heart! no one needs your passionate
suffrage to select this glory,
this is our lordly Hudson hardly flowing
under the green-grown cliffs.

"Driver! has this a peer in Europe or the East?"
"No no!" he said. Home! home!
be quiet, heart! this is our lordly Hudson
and has no peer in Europe or the East,

this is our lordly Hudson hardly flowing
under the green-grown cliffs
and has no peer in Europe or the East.
Be quiet, heart! home! home!

—PAUL GOODMAN, "The Lordly Hudson"

FROM THE
LIGHTHOUSE

Ay, thou art welcome, heaven's delicious breath!
When woods begin to wear the crimson leaf,
And suns grow meek, and the meek suns grow brief,
And the year smiles as it draws near its death.
—WILLIAM CULLEN BRYANT, "October"

Chapter One

AUTUMN USED TO BE MY FAVORITE TIME OF YEAR. I don't like it so much anymore. It's lost some of its luster. Autumn leaves on the Hudson weren't enough to make Ma stay. And what am I, compared to the bright yellow-orange-red of an October riverbank, the sun lighting up the sky, shining warm love on the whole entire earth? Not much: A knobby-kneed thirteen-year-old girl with black hair and the two biggest front teeth in the entire town of Hudson, New York. Foolish to think I could be enough to make Ma want to stay if the leaves couldn't.

The first months after Ma left were the hardest. Mostly because I kept expecting her to come back any minute. Thought I'd look out the window and there she'd be, rowing across the river in the punt, waving and shouting, "I'm back! Where's my little chickens?"

But that never happened.

It didn't stop me from waiting for her, though. I'd spend the day feeling like something was going to happen just up ahead, maybe after lunch or tomorrow morning. Like I'd written something on the calendar, set aside the day special, then forgotten what it was I was supposed to be ready for. To the outside world, it looked like I was polishing the brightwork or wiping

Clayton's nose or yelling at Sid. Sometimes I might have even looked happy. But inside, I was waiting. Always waiting.

Lunches and tomorrow mornings came and went like clockwork, but Ma never showed. So I waited. And while I waited, I thought about what I could have done to make Ma want to stay.

Sid and Rudy and I walked home from school together the day Ma left, just like we did every day. The leaves on the trees along the dirt road that leads to the river were beautiful. Every shade of orange, yellow, and red you could imagine burst from the treetops. The sun peeked through, making light and shadow patterns on the ground.

I was singing on the way home, as usual. I like to sing. I'm no Kate Smith, but I can carry a tune. I don't know how to explain it, really, but singing makes me happy. And it's a way of showing the inside of me to the world outside of me. If I'm happy, nothing shows it better than a happy song. And if I'm sad, there is nothing like a song to help me feel a little bit better.

Ma always said I would rather sing than talk, which I suppose is true.

"I don't know where you get it, Weezie," Ma used to say. "I can't carry a tune in a wheelbarrow."

That's not really true. Ma has a nice singing voice—high alto, just like me. We used to sing together, mostly in the kitchen. We might sing "Ain't We Got Fun" or the lollipop song while she was putting a meal together and us kids were around the table doing homework. I miss that.

Most people say that getting me to talk is like pulling teeth. Maybe so. But there's no sense in filling up the air with noise just for the sake of saying something. Some people think that if you don't say much you must not have anything interesting to say to begin with. I don't think that's true. I know quite a few people who talk constantly without having anything interesting to say at all. As Mr. Abraham Lincoln once said, it is better to remain silent and be thought a fool than to speak and remove all doubt.

I have lots of interesting things going on in my head. But I've found that a lot of times something that seemed terribly interesting or completely reasonable inside my head sounded pretty ordinary coming out of my mouth. Somehow the words get uncomfortable, awkward even, tumbling over my tongue.

It's different with singing. Perhaps because with singing, I know the words are right. Someone else has already chosen them and made them fit a certain mood or feeling. All I have to do is interpret them. Miss Kazmaier, our Glee Club director, calls it that—*interpreting*.

Sometimes I think maybe if I hadn't sung as much, Ma would have stayed. I was always singing something. Ma said she liked it most of the time, but once in a while she'd tell me to please give it just a tiny rest. Or she'd say that with all the boys' commotion plus my singing, she couldn't hear herself think.

Funny, but the boys' noise actually helps me hear myself think—brings it into sharper focus, I guess you could say. The louder and more boisterous my three brothers are, the calmer and more centered my own mind becomes.

Sometimes I'll be sitting in the parlor reading with the boys wrestling around me on the floor; Clayton bobbing in and out of range of Sid and Rudy's flailing arms and legs, shouting and squealing.

"Grab his leg, Rudy! Get him, Sid, get him!" Clayton doesn't care who wins, as long as they keep going at it so he can shout commentary and referee. Every once in a while, they'll pause to have Clayton give a ruling on some dispute.

"You're grabbing round the neck!"

"Was not—what's the ref say?"

Clayton will give his opinion in a giddy shriek, then Sid and Rudy will be back on the floor in a tumble of grunts and grabbed shirtsleeves. Then Ma or Dad will come into the parlor and holler for them to be quiet, and suddenly I'll realize they had been making a lot of noise. Their noise seems to have more presence in its absence, as if it left an actual empty space in the air when it is gone. I'd have to stop my reading and look around to see what had suddenly interrupted me. It was the quiet.

I've always been like that—Dad says that even as a baby I was kind of an island unto myself. Maybe that's why I like living in the lighthouse. It's also an island unto itself; calm and strong amid the noise and bluster of the world outside.

In any case, I was singing a Glee Club song as we walked home from school the day Ma left. I was practicing for my solo in the fall concert. It's a song called "Smiles."

"There are smiles that make us happy,
There are smiles that make us blue,
There are smiles that steal away the teardrops
As the sunbeams steal away the dewwwwww!"

I stretched my arms up to the sun and stood like a singer onstage waiting for applause. Sid and Rudy just kept walking.

I hurried to catch up behind Sid and sang to the back of his head.

"And the smiles that fill my life with sunshine
Are the smiles that you give to me!"

He ducked away and swatted at me with his hand. "Get off, Louise! I'll take ahold of you!"

I sighed. Sid has no sense of humor at all.

Chapter Two

WE CROSSED THE RAILROAD TRACKS and walked to the
river's edge. The Hudson lay before us, reaching out to each side
in a wide, majestic ribbon of gray-green water. Our home, the
lighthouse, sits in the channel to guide ships around the Middle
Ground Flats. My father, Owen Bloom, is the lighthouse keeper.

Usually someone was there to greet us and row us across the
river back to the lighthouse. Today only the punt greeted us,
pressed against the shore by the river current. We figured Dad
or Ma must have rowed across and gone into town for something.

"Should we wait?" asked Rudy.

"Nah. I'll row you across, then come back," said Sid.

We got in the punt and Sid started rowing crosscurrent.
Clayton was sitting on the deck of the lighthouse, legs dangling
over the edge. He had his head poked through two rails of the
iron deck fence, his hands clasped around a rail on each side of
his neck. Clayton's the baby, five years old. Born in 1933, the
year of the New Deal: A chicken in every pot.

"How's that little chicken in your pot, Myra?" Dad would
ask, Ma walking around big and swollen, belly arriving everywhere a few steps ahead of her. Clayton was the first Bloom kid
to be a chicken.

Then Ma started calling us all her chickens. Said she had enough chickens in her pot, thank you. Guess maybe she had one too many chickens. Maybe it's Clayton's fault she left.

So there was Clayton, nose running as usual. He's allergic.

"Hey, Clayton!" Rudy yelled. Clayton didn't holler back. Usually he does; he yells and hoots and hollers when anybody comes across the river. Not this time. Guess that should have given us a clue that something was wrong.

He watched us tie the punt to the ladder, climb out, and clank up the rungs, shoes scraping and the boat trying to pull the rope free and cruise down to Poughkeepsie with the current. Clayton just stared at us, wiping his snotty nose on the sleeve of his shirt.

"What's got into you?" said Sid, cuffing him on the shoulder. "You sick?"

Clayton took a noisy snuffle through his nose and swallowed. "Ma's gone."

"Where'd she go?"

"To market?" I asked. I was still humming "Smiles" under my breath.

Clayton shrugged. He looked up at me. "Is she gonna come back, Weezie?"

"What are you talking about, Clayton? 'Course she's coming back." I took one corner of the hankie that was pinned to his shirt and pinched it over the end of his nose. "Blow."

Sid gave a little laugh. "She's gotta cook supper, don't she? I'll tell Dad I'm going to row back and wait for her." He cuffed Clayton's shoulder again and went into the lighthouse, Rudy right behind him.

"Come on inside," I said. I took Clayton's hand and pulled him up.

Inside the lighthouse, Dad was sitting at the kitchen table, the keeper's log open in front of him. He was hunched over the book, writing with his fountain pen.

"Hey there, Dad," said Sid. Dad kept writing without looking up.

"Where's Ma?" asked Rudy. Dad didn't say anything, just kept writing. Like this particular entry in his logbook was the most important thing in the world. He put down his pen and closed the book, then smoothed the cover with his hand.

"Myra's gone," said Dad. He was talking to the smooth brown leather of the logbook cover. "Your ma's gone."

"Yeah, Clayton told us," said Sid. "I'll go back ashore and wait with the punt."

Dad ran his hand over his face and glanced up at us. He looked tired. "She's gone," he said. "Took off. Doesn't need a ride back."

My throat suddenly tightened. "Took off for where?" I asked.

Dad looked at me and shook his head like he didn't understand what I was asking. His eyes slipped away from mine toward the little icebox by the sink.

"Damned if I know," he muttered to the icebox.

"Ow, Weezie, you're hurting me." Clayton squirmed and tried to pull his hand from my grip.

I let his hand drop. I could feel my heartbeat at the back of my throat. I swallowed to try and quiet it.

"She's coming back, ain't she, Dad?" asked Rudy.

"Isn't she," I corrected Rudy faintly. I didn't need to hear Dad's answer because I already knew what it would be.

"I don't believe so, boy," said Dad.

In the silence that followed, my father's words floated upward and vanished into the top of the lighthouse, and I began to wait for a mother who would never return.

Chapter Three

"I'M HUNGRY," SAID CLAYTON. He ran the back of his hand under his nose. "Ma said she was going to make a cake."

"She can't make a cake if she's not here, can she?" said Sid. He walked out of the kitchen. His footsteps banged down the short hallway then up the stairs. A sudden harsh thud and scrape, then a metallic clank sounded through the floorboards as Sid kicked his bed against the wall.

The four of us still in the kitchen listened silently, looking around like we were seeing everything for the first time. The pretty cotton-print curtains on the window, the shiny stainless steel of the sink. The icebox made a dripping sound. The squeak of bedsprings as Sid sat down followed soon after. There aren't many things that are private in the close confines of the lighthouse.

"I'll make a cake, Clayton," I said. I bent down and wiped his nose again. "Ma can have a big piece with us when she gets back." I carefully kept my head turned away from Dad when I said the last.

My gaze landed on the front door of the coal stove with the word *perfect* across it in raised letters.

I could remember Ma standing at the stove making her chocolate cake. All of us kids were sitting at the kitchen table, and I

was singing—another Glee Club song, "Ain't We Got Fun"—
Ma was humming along and stirring the batter in time to the
tune.

"Can I stir some, Ma?" asked Clayton. Ma nodded.

"Ev'ry morning," I sang. "Ev'ry evening, ain't we got fun?"

Ma passed the spoon to Clayton and held the bowl low so he
could stir. She joined in and then we were all singing while
Clayton wrestled the big spoon in the bowl of batter.

"Not much money,
Oh but honey,
Ain't we got fun?"

"She took off for shore," said Dad, pulling me back to the
present. "Left me here yelling to her from the railing."

Ma was gone and suddenly it felt like we'd never have fun
again.

"I yelled, too," said Clayton. His chin trembled.

"You should have stopped her," said Rudy.

Dad stood up from the table. "She's a grown woman." He
picked up the logbook and walked out of the kitchen. I started
humming "Ain't We Got Fun" to try and bring Ma back.

I walked to the stove and began putting paper in the firebox.
I lit the paper with a match and put several sticks on top. Ma
glided across my mind, rowing away in the punt. I stopped
humming.

"Get me some coal, Clayton." It came out a bit rougher than
I intended. Clayton shuffled over and handed me several pieces
of coal from the sack next to the stove. I placed them one by one

on top of the little paper fire. I sighed and banged the lid of the firebox shut.

"That'll take a while to heat up," I said. Clayton nodded.

I headed into the pantry to get the cake ingredients.

"I need help, Clayton." I scowled at the boxes and bags of dry goods lining the pantry shelves. A box of Quaker cornmeal sat there dumbly, waiting for Ma to pick it up and tell it what to become: johnnycake or fritters or some coating on fish. It made me want to scream. Instead I turned to Clayton as he stepped around the corner and moved my mouth into a smile. "Come carry some things."

"Can you make that chocolate cake like Ma makes?" asked Clayton.

I handed him a can of cocoa. "Ma's got the recipe written down somewhere. We'll find it."

I walked back out to the kitchen and took Ma's *Fannie Farmer* off the shelf by the sink and began to leaf through it. There were grease spots on some of the pages. Recipes cut from the newspaper or written on scraps of paper were stuck randomly between the pages. They stuck out from the top like bookmarks.

As I leafed through the book, one of them fell out and floated to the floor. I picked it up and read a recipe for fish chowder written in Ma's neat handwriting. It was hard to believe that Ma had ever needed a written recipe for fish chowder. We had chowder at least once a week, all year round, made from canned milk and fish pulled from the river.

"Guess she was tired of fish," I said to the recipe. I looked over at Clayton standing by the stove with the box of cocoa in his hand. Rudy was still standing by the table holding his schoolbooks.

I tucked the chowder recipe back into the cookbook. "Ma went up to Albany for a nice dinner, is all. She'll be back by bedtime."

I motioned at Rudy with the cookbook. "So you better get your homework done."

He looked at me, his face blank. I waved the cookbook again. "Go on, sit down. You know the rules: homework done before play or chores. We're not going to fall apart just because Ma is gone for the afternoon." Rudy looked at me again, then over at Clayton. He pulled out the chair that Dad had been sitting in and slowly sat down. I waited until he took a pencil out of his pocket before I looked back at the cookbook.

"Here's the recipe, Clayton. I knew it was in here," I said.

Clayton came over and bent his head over the cookbook. "Does it say 'Ma's Chocolate Cake'? I want Ma's chocolate cake."

"It says 'Eggless Chocolate Cake,' which is the one Ma makes," I said. "Wait a minute." I walked over to the table. "I need the pencil for a second, Rudy."

Rudy grunted and handed me the pencil. I put the cookbook on the table and with the pencil made a line through the word *Eggless* and wrote *Ma's* above it.

"There," I said, handing the pencil back to Rudy. I held the cookbook out for Clayton to see. "Now it says 'Ma's Chocolate Cake.'" I put the cookbook on the table and sat down to do my homework while the oven heated. Clayton sat beside me, galloping a tin horse over the cocoa can and the saltshaker.

Dad walked back into the kitchen. "You'll have to make supper, Weezie," he said. "Think you can handle that?"

I nodded. "Guess so." I was used to helping Ma out in the kitchen.

Dad nodded. "Thank you, Louise."

"The rest of you kids are going to have to pick up the other things that Ma did around here," said Dad. "If we all work together, we can make a go of it." He looked up at the ceiling, toward where Sid was sitting on his bed. "We'll be fine if we all pull together."

"We can make it through one afternoon," I said. "Ma'll be back before long, Dad. She wouldn't just leave us."

Dad looked at me. I watched the scowl lines between his eyebrows quiver and deepen.

"Louise—" I pressed my hands against the table and waited for what he was going to say. *Times are bad and getting badder,* whispered a voice in the back of my head. *Ain't we got fun?*

Dad closed his eyes and sighed. When he opened his eyes again, the scowl lines were gone.

"You're right, Weezie—we can make it through one afternoon." He turned to walk down the hallway, his voice echoing off the plaster walls. "We'll make it through one afternoon at a time."

Chapter Four

"YOU SAID MA WOULD BE BACK BY BEDTIME," mumbled Clayton. I leaned over and tucked the blanket up under his chin. The October sun had set long ago, and the half-eaten chocolate cake, covered with a dishtowel, sat on a shelf in the pantry. My first attempt at dinner—canned beans and leftover chicken from the icebox—had turned out pretty well. Although I suppose Ma had really made it, not me.

"You're right. I did," I said. "She must have been delayed. Maybe the train is running late, or she didn't have enough money for the bus, so she had to walk to the train station."

"Or maybe it's raining in Albany," said Clayton.

I nodded. "Rain would certainly slow her down."

The metal bed creaked as Rudy leaned over the edge of the upper bunk to look down on us. "Rain wouldn't slow her down," he said. "I think she got drunk and is too embarrassed to come home."

"Rudy!" I stood up and faced him. "Don't say such a thing."

"It's true," he said. "She felt bad about leaving and drank too much liquor to forget her troubles, and now she's embarrassed to come home."

I thought of Ma in the sitting room downstairs, sipping a glass of wine at night and listening to the radio while Dad worked on inventory sheets or the logbook. I'd never seen her drunk. One night she'd gotten up from the sofa and put down her glass of wine. Her feet were moving on the little rug in time to the Benny Goodman Orchestra.

"Dance with me, Owen," she said.

Dad had looked up from his inventory and smiled.

"You know how I feel about dancing," he said.

Ma cocked her head and reached out her hand and wiggled her fingers.

"Come here, Owen; leave that old inventory and dance with your wife."

"I don't feel like dancing." Dad was scowling now.

"I'll have to find another partner, then," said Ma. Her voice was light and teasing.

"Suppose so," said Dad. He got up. "I've got a wick to check. I'll dance on upstairs."

Ma turned away. "Sid?"

"Huh?" Sid didn't look up. He was concentrating on tying a tuft of rabbit hair to the end of a bright green shad dart he'd been working on all evening. When Sid wasn't fishing, he was preparing to fish: buying tackle, digging worms, cleaning reels, or making shad darts.

Ma sighed and reached over to pull Sid from his chair. "It's high time you learned to dance, young man."

"But, Ma—"

"But nothing. I already got turned down once this evening, Sidney. Don't break my heart."

So Ma and Sid had danced while Dad checked the wick.

Clayton snuffled. "I don't care if she is drunked," he said. "I just want her to come home." He started to cry quietly.

I sat back down on the bed. "Ma's not drunk; Rudy's just making stuff up. Don't cry, Clayton. Ma's coming back. Don't cry."

Dad's footsteps sounded on the stairs coming down from the light tower.

Dad looked into the room and his eyes settled on Clayton, whose tears where sliding down toward the pillow. "Not a lot of good crying's going to do, Clayton," said Dad. He didn't say it unkindly, just matter-of-fact.

Clayton nodded but kept snuffling anyway. I picked his dirty shirt up off the floor and gave it to him to blow his nose on.

Dad stepped to the bed and put his hand on Rudy's shoulder. A light odor of kerosene came with him. "Good night, son."

"Good night, Dad."

Then he bent down and patted Clayton's face. "Good night to you, too, Clayton. You get some sleep."

Clayton held the dirty, snotty shirt in a crumpled ball against him like a blanket. He nodded.

"Things'll look better in the morning," said Dad. He patted Clayton's face again. "We're still a family. Nothing can change that." He turned back toward me. "Guess you better get into bed yourself, Louise."

"Yes, Dad. Good night."

He kissed the top of my head. I breathed in the kerosene and coal-smoke smell of him as he leaned in close. It brought a sudden lump to my throat. I didn't dare speak for fear I'd cry.

Chapter Five

I WENT INTO MY ROOM and got changed for bed, but I didn't get in. I stood still by the side of the bed, listening. I heard Dad walk down the stairs. The rattle and clank of the light works thumped through my bedroom wall adjoining the light tower.

I stepped into my slippers and walked down the hallway to Ma and Dad's room. I knew I shouldn't be snooping, but I needed to see if Ma had left anything behind. That would tell me if she planned on coming back.

I stood in the doorway looking for signs that Ma wasn't completely gone. The bed was neatly made, the quilt on top smooth and silent. The dresser was bare. Ma's silver hairbrush was gone. I walked to the dresser and ran my hand over the top. Ma's hand mirror was gone, too, the one she used to check her hair after she finished putting it up with pins. All the things I'd watched her handle and use a hundred times—the comb, the fat tortoise-shell hairpins she used to hold her long hair in a French twist— all gone.

I pulled open a couple of drawers. The top two were empty. The bottom one had Dad's shirts and pants. I pushed it shut with a grunt and stared at the dresser top.

Of course it made sense that Ma would take her brush and other hair things. That didn't mean she wasn't coming back. I looked under the bed and made out a pair of work boots, one on its side. A dust bunny drifted across the floor toward me as I moved my arm.

The only place left to look was the closet. I opened the door and looked in. Half a dozen empty wire hangers dangled from the rod. Dad's Lighthouse Service uniform hung mutely to one side, waiting to be called to duty. Nothing of Ma's. I inhaled, trying to smell her somewhere in the hollowness of the empty closet. There was nothing of her left. I started to close the door, then noticed a pale shape in one of the back corners.

I squatted down to grab it. It was a hat. A straw cloche hat— the kind that fits low on your head when you wear it. It had a little turned-up brim all around.

I moved out into the fantail of light near the hallway to get a better look. The front of the hat was covered with crumpled pink flowers. The fabric blossoms were sewn on closely together: pale pink petals around darker pink centers. They looked like cosmos or some kind of fantastic pansy. A braid of dark pink straw zigzagged across the back of the hat like a vine coming from the garden of flowers on the front. A hat full of blooms.

I could tell that the hat was old—not many people wore cloche hats anymore, even in Hudson, New York. I pulled the hat down onto my head and walked to the dresser. The hat hugged my head like a comforting hand. I looked at myself in the mirror. The brim came down to my eyebrows.

My blue eyes blinked back at me from under the rioting garden of pink flowers. Was this how Ma had looked when she wore this hat? I didn't remember ever seeing her wear it, but it had to be hers.

I turned my head and tried to look at myself out of the corners of my eyes. How many times had Ma worn this hat? Why had she kept it in the closet but never taken it out to wear? She must have gotten it when she was younger. I wondered if someone gave it to her or if she had bought it for herself.

I sighed and reached up to touch the flower petals. My head felt warm and snug inside the hat. I felt protected, like I was hiding from the rest of the world under it.

"I'll wear it till she gets back," I murmured to myself. "It'll be safe that way."

Back in my room, I took the hat off and put it in the rocking chair by my bed. That way I could see it when I was lying down. I snuggled under the covers and looked at the hat.

Even if I had only found one thing of Ma's, I told myself, and even if it was just an old straw hat, she'd left something behind, and that just might mean she intended to return home someday.

Later, something woke me. I stared through the darkness at Ma's hat on the rocking chair. Sleep wouldn't come. I couldn't turn my mind off. I rolled over, away from the hat, and sighed.

Voices floated down the hall from Sid's room. It was Dad and Sid. It reminded me of other late nights listening to Ma and Dad argue while I tried desperately not to hear.

Sid's voice suddenly rose in a shout. I felt my heart thump against my chest. I blinked my eyes at the dark window and strained to make out Sid's words. The lighthouse beam flashed across the top of the window, making me squint. Dad's voice was calm and slow, but Sid's replies were rapid and loud. Dad's voice rose to meet Sid's, and I could hear his words clearly.

"Don't speak of your mother that way!"

I yanked at my pillow and put it over my head. The cold of the sheet where my pillow had been made me shiver.

Sid was silent. I listened to the familiar sound of the bedroom door closing on its squeaky hinge. There were sounds from Sid's room as he climbed into bed, and then all was quiet. I stared at the straw cloche hat, its pink flowers made gray in the dim light.

"Hurry home, Ma," I whispered to the crumpled garden of petals. "You left lots of things behind."

Chapter Six

MA DIDN'T COME HOME IN THE NIGHT. The next morning, going to school, all I could think was that Ma was gone, but the rest of the world just kept right on as if nothing was different. It seemed impossible, but the river was just the same, the water a rippling gray-brown blanket spread out to each side until it was lost behind a curve of land. The sun shone down and the October leaves called out in their rust-colored voices, untouched by Ma's absence.

We climbed in the punt and Dad rowed us across to shore just like he had the day before. The oars creaked against the metal oarlocks and the water dripped off the ends of the oars, each droplet embraced and carried away by the river current.

We walked into town, across First Street and up toward the center of town. We turned down Fourth Street at Shufelt's Market. After two more blocks, Rudy and I turned into the Fourth Street School, and Sid walked across the next block to the new high school on Harry Howard Avenue.

Ethel Baskin met me at the door to homeroom. She clutched her books against her chest and leaned forward to stop me as she spoke. "Are you all right, Weezie? I heard your mom is gone."

A jolt of alarm hit me in the stomach. How did Ethel know already? Her mother was the postmistress in town and knew everyone's business. Including mine, I guessed. I tried to step around Ethel, but she moved in front of me and put her hand on my shoulder. Perhaps she meant it to be comforting.

"I'm so sorry," she said, her eyes round and wet with concern.

"What happened?" Gertrude Schouten had appeared next to Ethel. As always, she was searching for bad news.

Ethel put a protective arm around my shoulder. "That's Weezie's business, Trudy," she said. "If she wants to tell you, she will."

"Oh, Weezie, what happened?"

"Nothing happened," I said, brushing my hand against the brim of Ma's straw hat. "Nothing at all."

"Now, Weezie, there's no need to shoulder this burden all by yourself. That's what friends are for. To help in times of trouble." Ethel turned back toward Trudy and spoke in a dramatic stage whisper. "Weezie's mother left."

"Left?" echoed Trudy.

Ethel nodded importantly, the bearer of tragic news. "No note, no good-bye, just left."

Trudy put her hand to her mouth in horror. Suddenly there was a cluster of girls around me, all sighing and "oh-mying" in desperate concern over my runaway mother.

"I'm so sorry, Weezie."

"What can we do?"

"You poor thing."

I felt my face burning and looked down at the top of my math book. These were my friends. I had known most of them all my life, but right now all I wanted to do was get away from them.

"She's coming back!" I said, my voice rising.

We were interrupted by the sound of Mrs. Carney's hand-bell signaling for attention. "Louise Bloom, is that your voice I hear? I'm surprised at you." I was mortified that Mrs. Carney had had to speak to me. I really liked her. She was a no-nonsense woman who came to school every day in a black skirt, white blouse, and cardigan sweater. I considered her very sensible and scholarly because she didn't wear the floral housedresses that Ma and most of the other women I knew always wore.

I wanted to be a teacher one day, wearing sensible skirts and cardigan sweaters and a little felt hat with ribbon around the brim. I would teach in a town somewhere along the Hudson River and come home to the lighthouse every holiday.

"I'm sorry, Mrs. Carney."

Mrs. Carney nodded. "Seats everyone, please." I hurried toward my seat, face aflame, heart racing. From behind me, I heard a whisper. "Can you imagine your mother leaving? Mine would never do such a horrible thing."

"And did you get a load of that hat?"

I sat down at my desk. I could feel my throat contracting as I tried to swallow the lump that had lodged just behind my tongue.

Somehow I managed to get through the school day, avoiding conversation whenever possible. At least that wasn't unusual for me. Most people expected me to be quiet.

The final period of the day was activity period. There were all kinds of things to do during activity period: the school newspaper, gymnastics, citizenship class, Key Club, Drama Club, Future Farmers of America, Future Homemakers of America. I was in the Glee Club.

I walked to the Glee Club room with Eva Masterman. Eva

was the one friend who hadn't mentioned my mother once all day. I was grateful for her kind silence.

I took my place on the riser next to the other altos. The seventh- and eighth-grade Glee Club chorus is a really great chorus. I'm not being boastful—I've heard some people say that we are even better than the high school chorus. It's because of Miss Kazmaier. She knows more about singing than anyone I've ever known. And she loves it. You can see it on her face when we are singing. Sometimes when we hold a crescendo note, and her hands are held high above her head—telling us to "hold, children, hold that note"—and the harmonies flow and roll out into the air and into all the corners of the room, I can see the perfection in the note illuminated in Miss Kazmaier's face. It shines through her eyes and leaks out of her smile like a soft, flowing light. During those notes, those few seconds when all our voices are in perfect unison and vibrating harmony, it is easy to believe that everything in the entire universe is just exactly as it should be: perfect and good and full of grace. That's when goose bumps crawl up my arms and creep in a wonderful shiver across my back.

I really needed to feel that harmony right now. I wanted to erase the embarrassment and anger of trying to explain that my mother wasn't gone for good and that no one had to feel sorry for me. No one at all.

I had been chosen to do a solo in "Smiles." We were rehearsing for our fall concert to be held at the end of November, "A Celebration of American Music."

"We'll rehearse the program as it will be done at the concert," said Miss Kazmaier. "Soloists, be ready for your cues."

"What's with the old-lady hat?" asked Elwyn Fatherly behind me.

"You hush, Elwyn," whispered Eva from beside me.

Miss Kazmaier raised her hands, and we were all silent. She began the count, and we were singing. The first song on the program was "You're a Grand Old Flag," followed by "Yankee Doodle Dandy" and two other patriotic songs. The part of the program where I got to sing my "Smiles" solo came near the end. Our grand finale was "America the Beautiful."

But I couldn't keep my mind on the songs today. It kept wandering to missing Ma and wondering where she was. Every song—the patriotic ones, the happy ones, and the pretty ones—all made me feel sad. I even missed my cue for the solo. I had an ache inside me that seemed to get bigger with each note I sang.

Someone else's words set to music had always served me well—but now the words were all wrong. For the first time that I could ever remember, I didn't feel like singing. The harmony was gone. Singing wasn't fun anymore.

When rehearsal was over, I stayed to talk to Miss Kazmaier. "Yes, Louise, what can I do for you?"

I swallowed and tried to look at Miss Kazmaier, but the best I could do was to look at the collar of her blouse. "I'm switching activities," I said.

"Excuse me?" She tilted her head down and forward to hear me better.

"I—well, I'm switching activities," I said. "I'm not doing Glee Club anymore."

"What?" asked Miss Kazmaier softly. "I thought you enjoyed Glee Club, Louise. This is your third year!"

"I know."

"You've always had such a talent for singing," Miss Kazmaier kept going. "And the group is counting on you for the concert solo."

"You really shouldn't count on me, Miss Kazmaier. I miss a lot of school in the winter. When the ice gets bad."

"But, Louise, you enjoy it so," she said. Her forehead was all wrinkled up and her voice was quavery, like she had something in her throat.

I shook my head. "I don't want to do it anymore."

"Is it the solo?" she asked. "Someone else can do the solo." The more Miss Kazmaier tried to convince me to stay, the more I knew that I didn't want to sing in the Fourth Street School Glee Club one more minute.

"Please don't quit, Louise. I would hate to lose you." Those words, *I would hate to lose you*, nearly did me in. I knew if I stayed and tried to talk anymore about it, I would cry.

"I'm sorry, Miss Kazmaier." I turned and left.

Miss Kazmaier and the Glee Club would just have to make do without me.

Like I was trying to make do without Ma.

Chapter Seven

"WHY DO YOU THINK MA HASN'T COME HOME YET?" asked Rudy. It was our turn to polish the Fresnel lens that magnified the kerosene lights. It was a daily job. Kerosene smoke blackened the lens every night, and every morning it was cleaned off again. We were up in the top of the light tower, fifty feet above the water. Ma had been gone two weeks.

I stopped rubbing with my chamois cloth and looked out over the river. I could see the spires of the churches in Hudson City and, behind them, the distant shapes of the mountains.

I stood and listened, holding my breath so I could hear the river down below. Its steady sighing hum held me close, as it always had, and whispered its song to me.

I sent out a silent wish to the river, then. *Call her home,* I begged. *Make Ma come back to the lighthouse.* I hoped Ma could hear the river's voice like I could. I hoped she would hear it calling to her and come back to us.

"She's shopping," I said. "Someplace really nice. New York City or Boston. She took the train."

"What's she shopping for?"

"For us, silly," I said. I turned back to the lens and began rubbing furiously. "She's buying clothes and toys and lots of wonderful things. She's going to bring them with her when she comes back." I looked over at Rudy and smiled. "Like Christmas, only better. Because she'll be back long before Christmas. By Halloween at the latest."

"Where'd she get the money, Weezie?" asked Rudy. He had stopped polishing and stood looking at me, the cloth hanging limp in his hand.

I ignored his question. "Maybe she'll get you a Tom Mix gun or a Roy Rogers comic book." I paused again in my polishing and looked down at the riverbank, straining to see Ma's figure emerge from the trees. I knew she would appear if I watched carefully enough.

Rudy snapped the polishing cloth against the lantern-room windowsill. "I don't care about toys, anyway," he said. "I just want Ma to come back."

"You're pathetic."

I whirled around. Sid had come up while we were talking. His head and shoulders poked up through the trapdoor in the floor of the light housing. He shook his head. "Shopping." Sid said the word as if it was the dumbest thing he had ever heard in his life.

"You don't know anything about it, Sid," I said.

"I know enough to know that Ma isn't coming back." He hoisted himself up to the floor and kicked the trapdoor shut. "No matter what happy little stories you dream up."

It took every ounce of strength I had not to slap him across the face with my polishing cloth. "She's coming back!" My voice echoed in the lantern room. "Ma loves it here! She's coming back."

Sid crossed his arms and leaned toward me, his face stony. "No—you love it here, Louise. Ma didn't."

I looked away, across the river toward the town.

But instead of the town, I saw Ma waving from the bow of a boat down on the river. She and Clayton had gotten a ride from our friend Mr. Tomlinson in his new Chris-Craft motorboat. They were cruising slowly by the lighthouse, with Ma standing in the front waving to us. I could see a broad smile on her face as she looked up to the deck railing where I was standing.

"Ahoy, Louise!" Ma's hand made big, arcing swoops above her head.

"Ahoy, Ma! Hi, Clayton!"

"This is the life!" shouted Ma. "Tell your father I'm going to Poughkeepsie. I'll be back by morning!"

She laughed and turned away to look across the bow of the boat as they slowly moved down the river. 'Course she didn't go to Poughkeepsie. She was only joking, and Mr. Tomlinson dropped her and Clayton off a few minutes later.

"That was just the cat's pajamas," said Ma as she climbed up the ladder after Clayton. Her face was flushed and her hair, black like mine, swirled in little windblown wisps around her face. I remember thinking that she looked beautiful standing there on the deck with her messy hair and cheeks red from the wind on the river.

I rubbed my cloth against a black smudge along the bottom of the lens. I didn't want to believe that Sid was right, but hard as I tried, I couldn't shake the memory of how happy Ma had seemed standing with her back toward the lighthouse as that shiny Chris-Craft chugged farther and farther away.

Chapter Eight

I WAS IN THE KITCHEN peeling potatoes for dinner. Rudy was doing his homework at the table, and Clayton was trying to wash the kitchen windows. Even standing on a chair, he couldn't reach high enough to get the top of the windowpanes, so Rudy kept getting up to help.

Dad and Sid had gone up to the light tower to check the wick and fill the kerosene. We heard the loud clank of gears as they wound the works that rotated the light. There was comfort in the solid thudding of metal against metal as it vibrated through the house. The winding stopped with the muffled *tock* of the wheel chain resting against the cogs of the crank gear.

I heard sounds of arguing in the stairwell. Heavy footsteps thudded down the stairs then across the hallway. Sid burst into the kitchen and headed for the door.

Dad came stomping through the kitchen following Sid. "Don't walk away from me while I'm talking to you," said Dad.

Sid stopped but didn't turn around. "I ain't doing it," he said.

"Rudy's making the beds, Louise is cooking and keeping this kitchen up to snuff." Dad scowled and waved his hands at each of us kids as he spoke. "Even Clayton is dusting and polishing the brightwork! Look at him washing those windows." Dad reached out and turned Sid around to face him. The rest of us had stopped what we were doing to watch.

"I ain't doing it," repeated Sid. He looked at Dad sideways, his head half facing away.

Dad shook his head. "You don't have a choice, son. We've all got to work together to keep this family running. And clean clothes are a necessary part of keeping it running."

Sid shrugged. "Weezie can do it."

The anger came back into Dad's face. "Weezie is doing enough."

"I don't know how to run the machine," said Sid.

Dad grabbed Sid by the arm and pulled him toward the little room off the pantry where the washing machine was. "We can remedy that."

Sid jerked his arm out of Dad's grasp. "I know where it is," he said.

Rudy and I looked at each other as they left the room, then followed behind. I heard Clayton jump off the chair and scramble to catch up.

I stepped into the washing room. Sid was standing by the washing machine with his arms folded across his chest, his face set in a scowl. Because there was no electricity in the lighthouse, we had a gasoline-powered washing machine. Dad was showing him how to step on the kick pedal to get it running.

Dad straightened up from the machine. He motioned toward the clothes scattered on the floor and shouted over the sputtering engine. "Go to it."

Sid shook his head. I gasped.

Dad's face showed surprise, then his mouth tightened into a thin line. "Do the laundry, Sid."

"I ain't doing laundry!" said Sid.

"By the Jesus, you will do laundry!" said Dad, his voice rising higher.

"I'm going on sixteen!" shouted Sid. "I ain't doing woman's work!" He kicked at the clothes on the floor. "It's worthless woman's work, and I ain't doing it!"

Dad kicked off the machine. Face red with fury, the veins on his forehead bulging, Dad grabbed Sid by the shirt with both hands and shoved him against the wall. Sid's shoulders made a dull thudding noise as they hit the wall beside the washing machine. His eyes were round with surprise and fear.

Dad spoke through clenched teeth, his lips barely moving. His voice was low and deep with anger. "Don't you ever raise your voice to me," he said. He jolted Sid against the wall to emphasize the word *ever*. "Do you understand?"

Sid gave a tight nod. Dad released his grip on Sid and stepped back. He stared at Sid as he raised a hand toward the washing machine.

"Now I want you to get that washing machine going, and I want you to wash this family's clothes. You think you can do that, son?" Again Sid nodded. "Thank you," said Dad.

Dad turned and looked at the rest of us clustered together in the doorway. The color had drained from his face, leaving him ashen. The energy seemed to have left his voice as well, and he spoke in nearly a whisper. "The rest of you kids have chores to do. I suggest you get to them."

Rudy and Clayton scurried away, and Dad walked past me

through the doorway to follow them. I stayed and watched Sid begin to pick clothes up off the floor and fling them into the washing machine.

"If he thinks I'm sticking around here, he's crazy," Sid muttered. There was a tremble in his lower lip. "Ma had the right idea." He balled up a shirt and threw it hard into the washing machine.

"What are you talking about?" I said. Sid didn't answer, just kept picking clothes up off the floor. "Sid?"

"Go away, Louise," said Sid.

"But—"

"Leave me alone!"

I walked back to the kitchen. Clayton had already climbed back up on the chair. I heard Rudy sigh. I thought of Dad's face as he was holding Sid's shirt, and I knew it was a picture of what we all felt like inside: ugly and hurt and angry all at the same time. All us Blooms that Ma had left behind, wilting like pansies in a killing frost.

I turned on the radio. It ran off an old car battery, and we didn't listen to it often, but I felt the need for something cheerful just then. The Bert Lown Orchestra was playing live from the Biltmore Hotel in New York City. The stand-up singer's voice danced into the room. He was singing my solo song.

"There are smiles that make us happy,
There are smiles that make us blue,
There are smiles that steal away the teardrops
As the sunbeams steal away the dew."

Instead of making me happy, though, it nearly made me cry. I quickly reached over and turned it off.

The music left as if it had never even considered staying.

Chapter Nine

By mid-November we had gotten accustomed to our routine without Ma. The ache of missing her was still there, but we were functioning as a household. Rudy and Sid helped Clayton get ready in the morning. The rest of us took care of ourselves. Sid did a load of laundry once or twice a week without complaint. I did the cooking, and I was getting much better at it.

I wore Ma's hat all the time, except when I was sleeping. It had become a permanent accessory.

"Where'd you find that old hat?" asked Dad one morning before school.

I shrugged, embarrassed, and put a protective hand up to hold it on my head. "On the floor in Ma's closet."

Dad gave a little laugh. "Your mother had that when we were married—1921. Think she got it when she graduated from high school."

"Is it okay if I wear it, Dad?"

Dad looked up from his eggs. "Nobody else around here is going to wear it—are you, Sid?"

Sid rolled his eyes but didn't say anything.

"Rudy?"

"Nooooooo!" Rudy shook his head.

"Clayton, you want to wear that pretty pink hat?"

"Daddy!" shrieked Clayton. "It's a *girl's* hat!"

"Oh, guess it is." Dad took another bite of egg. "Besides, looks very pretty on you, Louise."

"Yeah," muttered Sid as he passed by me, too low for Dad to hear. "Pretty screwy."

I ignored Sid and took Clayton's empty plate from the table.

Clayton and Dad had become inseparable in the weeks since Ma had been gone. Clayton helped Dad do all his chores around the lighthouse: winding the works that rotated the light, checking and filling the kerosene, trimming the wick, fixing things up around the house. Dad took to calling Clayton his Right-Hand Man.

"Me and my Right-Hand Man are going down the cellar to the cistern," he'd say, and Clayton, looking very serious, would trail behind him down the narrow stairs to the cellar to check on the water supply. At supper every night, he'd tell us how Clayton had helped him that day. "Don't know what I'd do without my Right-Hand Man." Then he'd reach out and mess Clayton's hair.

For Clayton's part, he didn't like to let Dad out of his sight, even for sleeping. He usually woke up in Dad's bed in the morning. I would often wake at night to the sound of his bare feet padding down the hall to Dad's bedroom. He couldn't sleep without making sure Dad was still nearby.

Dad and Clayton stayed in the lighthouse during the day while the three of us older kids went off the school in Hudson City. Dad and Clayton would row us to shore in the morning and be waiting for us when we walked back to the river in the afternoon. Miss Kazmaier still stopped me in the hall once in a while to ask if I wanted to rejoin the Glee Club. I always told her I was enjoying the Future Homemakers of America.

"I'm helping out a lot more at home now," I said.

"Of course, Louise, I understand," said Miss Kazmaier.

The truth is, I still didn't have the heart to sing.

On the Friday before Thanksgiving, we headed in to school as usual. The river was still clear of ice, so we went across in the boat. Clayton was sitting on Dad's lap in the middle of the punt, his little mittened hands resting on Dad's legs as they waited for us to get in.

Sid had his school stuff in a knapsack. He threw it into the stern of the punt before hopping in.

"Going hiking, Sid?" asked Rudy.

"Going hiking, Sid?" Sid mimicked Rudy in a high-pitched voice.

Looking back on it, I suppose we should have known something was up. Sid never carried books back and forth to school. He was doing well on a day that he remembered a pencil, never mind a knapsack full of stuff.

But I was worrying about how I was going to manage my first Thanksgiving turkey, not what Sid was taking to school. Rudy was just annoyed, and Dad did his best to ignore the boys whenever they lit into each other. So no one thought much of Sid's knapsack.

The wind was coming down the river, blowing at us as Dad rowed toward shore. The gray sky hung low over the cold, choppy water and us. At the Hudson side of the river, the boat touched against the shore, and we all clambered out. Sid pushed the bow of the punt back into the current, and Dad and Clayton headed back to the lighthouse, rowing together.

"Bye!" called Clayton, taking his hand off an oar long enough to give a short wave.

"Bye!" Rudy and I stood onshore waving, then turned toward the town. Sid was already near the railroad track, walking quickly with long strides, his knapsack slung over one shoulder. He didn't look back to wave.

"Wait up, Sid!" Rudy called. We trotted to catch up.

As we crossed the double set of tracks, the toes of our shoes sent stones clanging against the rails.

There were usually men loitering by the empty boxcars, waiting for the train to begin moving so they could hop a ride to the next town, or maybe the one after that. They were "hoe boys," unemployed men wandering from place to place in search of work. Although the worst of the Depression was over and lots of people were back at work with President Roosevelt's job programs, there were still quite a lot of roving men looking for whatever work they might find. I shivered as we passed them, thinking about the cold and what a bleak thing it would be to ride in a boxcar in November. December and January would be even worse. I wondered where these men would spend Thanksgiving.

"Wouldn't want to be a hobo this time of year," muttered Rudy.

"You're a sissy, anyway," said Sid. "Knowing you, you're probably cold right now."

"Am not," said Rudy. He took his hands out of his jacket pockets.

I watched Sid cross the street, his pant legs slapping around his ankles in the November wind. Rudy and I joined the other kids walking up the stairs to the Fourth Street School.

Chapter Ten

AFTER LUNCH I ASKED MRS. CARNEY how to cook a turkey. During recess, she wrote out detailed directions for me, including a recipe for stuffing.

"You look these over," she said. "If you have any questions, you just let me know, Louise."

I took the piece of paper from her. "Thank you, Mrs. Carney."

She patted me on the shoulder. "Everyone cooks their first turkey sometime. You're doing it a little earlier than most. But you are a very bright girl; you'll do just fine."

After school, I met Rudy in the hallway outside his classroom. Ethel Baskin stopped us in the hall and said everyone missed me at Glee Club.

"It's a shame not to use that lovely voice of yours, Weezie," said Ethel. Somehow even when Ethel gave a compliment, it came out sounding like something else. I didn't know what to say, so I just said "Happy Thanksgiving." I missed everyone at Glee Club, too, but I didn't miss singing. I told myself that every day: I didn't miss singing.

Rudy and I walked across the street to wait for Sid. As I walked, I planned out the magnificent Thanksgiving dinner that I was going to prepare. It would be the most spectacular Thanksgiving dinner ever served in the lighthouse. I just knew that Ma would be home for Thanksgiving. What better time for a homecoming? She'd realize just how thankful she was to have us as a family, and she'd be pulled back to the lighthouse as surely as the moon pulled the tide. And when she came, I would be prepared.

I listed the menu in my head as Rudy and I crossed the street. Turkey, squash, johnnycake, rolls, peas, mashed potatoes, and mincemeat pie for dessert. I'd make homemade cranberry sauce and gravy, too. When Ma arrived home on Thanksgiving morning, she'd be overwhelmed with gratitude and love to think that I had, all on my own, prepared her a feast fit for a queen.

I pictured Ma standing in the kitchen staring down at the table laden with food. "My little Louise," she'd say. "You cooked this splendid meal for me?" We'd embrace and cry a little, but not too much to be maudlin. "I love you, Weezie," Ma would whisper into my ear as we held each other. "How could I have ever left you?"

And with the last bite of pie, as we all sat around the table sighing and groaning under the pleasant ache of stomachs stuffed with good food, Ma would wipe her mouth and look around the table at all our shining faces.

"I'll never, never leave you again," she'd say.

"Huh?" said Rudy.

I felt in my pocket for the paper that had Mrs. Carney's turkey instructions on them.

"I didn't say anything."

"Yes, you did," said Rudy. "You said 'never again,' sounded like."

I ignored him and walked faster. We were in time to hear the final bell echo inside the high school. Soon after, kids began to pour out of the front doors.

"Hi, Blooms." Sid's friend Baldy Hanscombe waved to us as he walked up and stopped in front of us. His given name was Norman, but his older brother had called him Baldy as a baby because he didn't have any hair, and the name had stuck. "How's Sid? He must be on death's door for your old man to let him stay out of school."

"He's not out of school, Baldy. We're waiting for him." I stated the obvious.

"You'll be waiting all day, then. He wasn't in school."

My heart began to flutter. "You must have missed him," I said. "He walked to school with us this morning, same as always."

Baldy stared dully at me. "His desk is right next to mine. He wasn't in school."

"Where'd he go?" I asked. Baldy looked at me blankly. I stared at him, trying to quell the panic that was rising inside me. "Tell us, Baldy."

Baldy shrugged his shoulders, his eyes wide. "I don't know! He didn't tell me anything."

I looked at the students walking past us on the sidewalk and knew that Sid wasn't going to come out of the school. "I didn't know," said Baldy. "You guys miss so much school in the winter. I thought it was early for ice to keep you out, but I didn't think anything of it. Neither did anyone else."

"There's no ice on the river, Baldy," said Rudy.

I ignored Baldy and turned to Rudy. "Come on, we've got to tell Dad."

I ran toward the river, Rudy at my heels.

Chapter Eleven

WE REACHED THE RIVER OUT OF BREATH and gasping. Dad and Clayton were just off shore, their backs to us as they rowed across the current.

"Dad! Dad!" I shouted. "Sid's gone!"

Dad twisted around in the boat as it bumped against the riverbank. "What?"

Rudy and I began talking at once.

"Sid's gone!"

"He wasn't in school—"

Scowling, Dad pulled the oars quickly into the boat and held up a hand. "Wait." He climbed out of the boat, helping Clayton out after him. He stood in front of us, looking at us intently. "Now tell me what is going on. Where's Sid?"

I looked at Rudy, then back at Dad. "Sid didn't go to school today. We saw Baldy, and he said Sid wasn't in school."

"And he had his knapsack this morning!" said Rudy. "Had it on his shoulder."

"Skipping school doesn't mean he's gone," said Dad. I saw his eyes wander past us toward the railroad tracks. "Just means he didn't go to school." He stepped back and hauled the boat up onto the riverbank.

I looked up at Dad. "He said Ma had the right idea."

Dad's head turned sharply toward me. "What?"

"By the washing machine. When you guys had the fight . . ." My voice trailed off and the last came out in a whisper. "He said Ma had the right idea."

"She didn't. Your ma didn't have the right idea." Dad took Clayton's hand. "Come on, we'll go find him."

The four of us walked quickly back across the railroad tracks and into town. There were still some kids on the sidewalk outside the high school. Baldy Hanscombe was not among them.

I watched Clayton's feet climb up the granite steps as I followed him and Dad into the building. One of his shoelaces was untied.

The principal's office was on the first floor. Our footsteps echoed on the wooden floorboards in the empty hallway.

"Mr. Bloom. Good to see you, sir," said Principal Wolcott.

"Mr. Wolcott," said Dad. He dropped Clayton's hand to clasp Principal Wolcott's. "I'm looking for Sid."

"Sid?" said Principal Wolcott. "He's not after school for anything, I don't believe." He walked into his office and stopped in front of the secretary's desk. "Mrs. Dunbar, is Sid Bloom after school today?"

Mrs. Dunbar looked at us, then shook her head. "He was absent today, Mr. Wolcott." She raised her eyebrows and looked at Dad and then back at Mr. Wolcott.

Mr. Wolcott cleared his throat. "Yes, well, I had been meaning to talk to you about that, Mr. Bloom," he said.

"You know why Sid was out today?" asked Dad.

"I don't know what we'll do if Sid misses as much school this winter as he did last," began Principal Wolcott. "I understand that you have an unusual situation, living in the middle of the river, but the State of New York does not look kindly on students missing twenty or thirty days of school a year, ice or no ice. And now with your wife gone . . ."

"Sid. Have you seen my boy Sidney today?" Dad repeated.

"No, sir," said Mr. Wolcott. "That's what I'm referring to. If this is the beginning of his usual winter attendance, it is simply not acceptable for—"

"Yes, sir, Mr. Wolcott, I understand," said Dad. "We'll talk about that real soon, I promise." He turned on his heel and walked quickly back down the hall, the three of us trailing behind him.

"Steps will have to be taken, Mr. Bloom," called Mr. Wolcott from behind us. "School attendance is mandatory!"

Dad didn't look back, but raised his hand in a final wave as we walked out of the building.

Dad was walking faster now, heading down the street toward Shufelt's Market. I took Clayton's hand and pulled him along as we tried to keep up.

Inside the market, Mr. Shufelt waved in greeting. "Hi, Owen, kids."

"Good afternoon to you, Steven," said Dad. "Have you seen Sid today?"

"I saw him this morning, as a matter of fact," said Mr. Shufelt. He smiled. "What kind of mischief has he gotten into now?"

"None that I know of," said Dad. "He didn't tell me where he was headed after school, is all."

"He didn't come in with the usual bunch after school," said Mr. Shufelt. "I expect he didn't want to put anything else on your credit."

"How's that?" asked Dad.

"He put a box of crackers and a stick of pepperoni on your credit this morning," said Mr. Shufelt. He glanced at us kids then back at Dad. "I hope that's all right, Owen. I assumed you knew about it."

Dad grunted and reached into his pocket. "How much?"

Mr. Shufelt looked in a little book beside the cash register. "Thirty-nine cents."

Dad counted the money out of his pocket and handed it to Mr. Shufelt. "Thank you, Steven."

Mr. Shufelt opened the cash drawer and dropped the coins in. "Told me he was headed to school. I figured maybe they were going on some kind of a nature hike, with that knapsack. You know Mr. Hisgan at the high school is real big into nature." He stopped and looked at Dad, who was kneading his chin between the thumb and forefinger of his right hand and staring at the floor.

Dad looked up and gave a tight smile. "Well, if you see him, tell him to head home."

"Sure thing, Owen." Mr. Shufelt nodded and winked at Clayton.

We walked back outside. Dad was already a block ahead of us by the time Rudy, Clayton, and I had stepped out onto the sidewalk.

"Dad?" I called as we trotted behind him along the sidewalk. "Dad!"

"I'm tired," said Clayton. His feet scuffed against the sidewalk as he tried to keep up with Rudy and me. I gripped his hand tighter so he wouldn't think about slowing down.

"We got to find Sid, Clayton," said Rudy.

Dad walked back toward the river. We followed along behind and came out of the trees facing the railroad tracks. Two boxcars, their maroon sides made dark in the overcast afternoon light, sat silently as we approached.

"He hopped a train," I said to no one in particular.

Dad looked back over his shoulder at me, then at the boxcars. He put his hand out, palm toward us. "You kids stay here." He walked toward a small group of men standing by the empty boxcars.

I kept hold of Clayton's hand as Dad walked to the boxcars. Two men where standing on the ground next to the open door of a boxcar that had ALBANY AND BOSTON stenciled on the side in white letters.

They talked for a while, Dad gesturing toward the lighthouse then back toward us kids.

"I'm glad Sid went," said Rudy.

He must have seen the shock in my face, but Rudy didn't flinch. He looked back at me without blinking. "How's Ma going to know we want her back if no one goes after her?"

I looked out at the lighthouse, standing silent and tall against the gray sky.

"She knows," I said. "How could she not?"

Dad came pounding back up to us from the track. "Come on, we're going to the lighthouse."

Clayton tried to sit in Dad's lap when we piled into the boat. "No, Clayton," said Dad. "You sit by Weezie."

Dad rowed across the river with short, hard strokes, as if he was angry at the water. "I'm going after your brother," he said.

No one spoke the rest of the way to the lighthouse.

Dad grabbed some extra money out of the jar in the pantry and put some bread and cheese in a satchel that he slung across his chest. He took the logbook down off its shelf in the kitchen and handed it to me.

"You've got to keep the log," he said. "Don't forget."

"Yes, Dad."

Rudy, Clayton, and I were huddled together in the kitchen as Dad paced around gathering the things he'd need on his search for Sidney.

Apparently satisfied that he had what he needed, he stood in front of us. He placed his hand on my shoulder. "Don't let the light go out," he said.

I nodded. "Yes, Dad."

He turned to Rudy. "Weezie's going to need your help, son."

"Don't you worry, Dad. We'll keep it lit. Nothing to it." He tried a smile, but I saw the quiver in his cheek.

Clayton had been whimpering since we had climbed up the ladder from the boat. Now, as Dad turned finally to him, he wailed and grabbed onto Dad. His arms and legs wrapped around Dad's leg, his eyes squinted in concentration as he held on as tightly as he could. Dad staggered and stepped back to steady himself. He didn't try to pull Clayton off just then.

"I got to go, Clayton."

"No," said Clayton, tears leaking out of the corners of his clenched eyelids.

"Yes, Clayton," said Dad gently. "There's just no getting around it."

"No," said Clayton. "No!"

"I'm coming back, son. You help your sister and brother keep things going around here. You're my Right-Hand Man."

Clayton shook his head, his eyes still closed.

Dad looked at me while he stroked Clayton's head. "I'll send Mr. Shufelt to stay with you." I nodded.

Dad reached down and untangled Clayton from around his leg. Clayton began to scream. "Don't go! Don't go!"

Dad held Clayton's arms and thrust him toward me. It took both Rudy and me to hold Clayton from running after Dad as we watched him go out the door onto the deck. "Don't go! Dad! Dad!" Clayton screamed.

Some of Clayton's panic began to creep up my spine, and I felt the need to watch Dad go. Rudy must've felt the same way, because we both started down the hallway. We had to walk stiff-legged as we dragged a struggling and screaming Clayton out onto the deck.

So that was how Dad left to find Sid, rowing across the river just like Ma, with Clayton there screaming at the railing. We stood and watched him go as Clayton's cries rose up from the concrete deck and flew out over the river like seagulls crying in the cold.

Chapter Twelve

WE STOOD THERE AND WATCHED until Dad climbed out of the boat onto shore. Clayton wasn't screaming anymore. It was like he'd used up all the fight he had in him trying to get Dad to stay. He was just hanging limp between Rudy and me, his arms bent at the elbows where we were gripping them, tipped up beside his ears like the legs on a crab.

I leaned over and wiped his nose with the handkerchief pinned on his coat. Rudy let go of Clayton's arm.

"Just us," said Rudy. His voice was raspy and low. "Supposed to be six Blooms, not three." He turned to go in to the lighthouse.

I put my hands under Clayton's armpits and hoisted him up onto my hip. I hadn't picked him up in a long time, not since he was two or three. My knees buckled a little, and I shifted him around a couple times until I had my balance back.

"You've grown, Clayton," I said, grasping for some small thing to make him happy. "You're getting to be a big boy."

"No, I'm not," said Clayton. His voice was small and still wet with crying. "I'm not a big boy."

I swallowed against the ache in my throat and felt my eyes start to sting with tears. I nodded at him. "Not big enough for all this, I don't suppose." I hugged Clayton closer and followed Rudy inside.

I cleaned Clayton's face up and pinned a new handkerchief to his shirt. I tossed the snotty handkerchief on the pile of clothes by the washing machine. Rudy was sitting at the kitchen table when I walked back in. He looked up at me and watched me walk across the floor. Clayton was standing in the middle of the room, his eyes glued to me.

"I'll be right back." I headed toward the back door.

"I'm coming!" said Clayton.

I shook my head. "I'm going to the privy, Clayton. I'll be right back." I steered him toward the kitchen table. "You sit right here with Rudy."

When I got back inside, they were still in the same position as when I had left. Just sitting there, staring at the table, the sink, the floor. They both turned to look at me as I walked into the kitchen. I could feel their eyes on me when I hung up my coat on the peg by the door and moved to the coal stove. I turned around to face them.

"I'm not in charge of you!" Rudy and Clayton were silent. "You don't have to wait for me to tell you what to do."

Rudy sighed and stood up, then sat back down again. Clayton began to cry again. He still didn't take his eyes off me, though.

"If you ain't in charge of us, Weezie, who is?" asked Rudy.

I looked at those two boys sitting at the table, and my heart sank. I wasn't ready to be a mother to them. And I would never be ready to be a mother to anyone if it meant someday leaving my kids on their own before they were ready. It would be better never to have kids than to someday leave them sitting at a kitchen table, staring at the empty spot where their mother should have been.

The lighthouse felt hollow and empty. The three of us scared and lonely kids just didn't fill it up enough to make it a home. It was like some kind of cavern where the echoes of the life we used to have with Ma were still rattling around inside, bouncing off the floor and the walls then back up to the very top of the light tower. When Dad and Sid were here, we had enough of us to absorb the echoes and keep them from ricocheting around us. Now that the two of them were gone, we could hear the echoes again, loud and clear.

The clock in the sitting room chimed four o'clock. It felt like midnight.

I looked back at the boys and decided Rudy was right. Someone had to be in charge. And I supposed it might as well be me.

"The first thing to do is get the fire going," I said. "Take this chill off."

"I'll do that!" said Rudy. He walked over to the coal stove and got to work on the fire.

I smiled at Clayton. "It'll be dark soon. We better light the wick, Clayton," I said. "I need someone who knows what they're doing up there."

Clayton sniffled and stared at me. "Guess that's me," he said.

"Guess it is." I took his hand and we walked up the spiral staircase to the light. In the lantern room, I opened the door on the Fresnel lens to get at the chamber that held the wick. I checked the fuel tanks and added kerosene. Then we lit the wick. Dad had a big brass lighting rod that could reach all the way in. After the wick, we secured the door to the lantern room and walked down the few stairs to the light works.

I grabbed the works handle with both hands and began to turn the crank. The wood of the handle was worn smooth from the hands of the light keepers who had wound these works over the sixty years since the lighthouse had been built. I turned the gear slowly, straining to lift the heavy chain and counterweights that, aided by gravity, pulled against the gears and turned the light.

"Let me help!" Clayton reached up to grasp the handle.

I pushed his hand away. "You're not tall enough, Clayton. Let me finish."

"Dad lets me do it!" He grabbed again for the handle just as I thrust my weight on top of it to crank it downward. The heavy iron arm of the crank handle hit Clayton on the bridge of his nose with a hollow thump as he bobbed upward to meet it.

Clayton let out a sharp cry then froze with his hands over his nose. I bent down, my heart thumping. "Are you all right?"

He shook his head.

"I'm so sorry, Clayton." I reached my arms around him to clasp him to me, but he drew back.

"Ow! Don't touch my nose!" He began to cry then, sobbing and whimpering.

"Let me see it." I pulled his hands from his nose, and the blood began to flow down his face and onto the front of his shirt. My heart flip-flopped. "Oh, Clayton."

We clumped down the rest of the stairs with me holding Clayton's elbow and him holding the front of his shirt bunched up against his bleeding nose.

Down in the kitchen, I grabbed a dishtowel and held it against his nose. "Ow! Ow!" he cried.

"What happened?" said Rudy.

"Weezie hit me with the crank!" howled Clayton.

"Shh. It's okay. You'll be okay. Just hold your nose." I fought to keep my voice steady. I patted Clayton's back and felt it rise and fall with his sobs. "You're okay, Clayton. It's just a nose-bleed. You'll be fine."

"I want Daddy and Ma."

"I know, Clayton. We all do."

"Why won't Ma come home?" His voice came out in little gasps between sobs.

I was silent. I didn't know the answer.

"Shhhh." I put my hand gently on Clayton's bowed head. "Don't worry about that right now. You sit tight." I tilted his head up and looked at his face. "Let me see your nose." I lifted the cloth. Blood immediately began to leak out of his nose. A dark bruise was beginning to spread over the bridge of his nose toward each eye. I replaced the cloth and guided his hand back on top of it. "Pinch it."

"I'll get another towel," said Rudy.

Clayton whimpered and bent his head back down over his lap. We stayed like that for a while, Clayton bent over in the chair and me standing beside him with my hand on his back. His crying had quieted.

"Why did Sid run away?" he asked. "Does he hate us?"

"No," I said quietly. "Sid doesn't hate us."

"Well I hate *him*. He made Dad leave."

He started to cry again. I hugged his shoulders against me.

"Towel," said Rudy. I took the old towel from Clayton and helped him get the new one on his nose. We stayed there in the kitchen, waiting for his nose to stop bleeding.

A knock on the front door made me look up. I left Clayton

on the chair holding his nose and walked to the door. Mr. Shufelt was standing on the deck. I stepped aside to let him in.

"Clayton's got a nosebleed," I said.

"Oh," said Mr. Shufelt. "What'd he get into?" He hurried into the kitchen and bent over Clayton, who started crying again.

"Weezie did it," he whimpered.

"It was the light-works crank," I said. "Clayton, you know it was an accident." My voice had a sharp edge to it, in order to cut through the thickness in my throat.

Mr. Shufelt gave me a little smile. "I know your sister, Clayton. She would never hurt you on purpose. Here. Let's see what that looks like."

He lifted the dishtowel away from Clayton's nose. It was no longer bleeding, but there was a nasty red welt on the top of his nose just between his eyes.

"You'll have a couple of nice shiners," said Mr. Shufelt. He reached out to ruffle the top of Clayton's head.

Mr. Shufelt straightened up. "I don't suppose you kids have had supper yet?"

"No, sir," said Rudy.

"How about some fried eggs?" asked Mr. Shufelt. "That's one thing I'm pretty good at making." He grabbed a frying pan from the wall beside the sink and banged it on top of the stove. "I see someone's done a good job getting a fire started."

"Yes, sir," said Rudy.

"Need some help here with these eggs, Clayton," said Mr. Shufelt. "How about it?"

Clayton looked up at me and then over to Mr. Shufelt. "Can I crack the eggs?" he asked.

Mr. Shufelt winked at me over the top of Clayton's head. "I was hoping you would," he said.

After supper, I walked Clayton upstairs and into bed. His eyelids drooped as he looked up at me.

"You try to get some sleep." I pushed the hair off his forehead.

He nodded and took a deep, wavering breath. "Weezie?"

"Yes, Clayton?"

"I know you didn't mean to hurt me. I'm sorry I said that."

"I know, sweetie. It's okay."

He gave a great heaving sigh. "And Weezie?"

"Yes, Clayton."

"Don't tell Sid what I said about him."

"I won't. I know you didn't mean it."

Clayton stared up at me. "Is that Ma's hat?"

I nodded.

"I wish she was here," he whispered.

"I know, sweetie. We all do."

I stayed there until Clayton closed his eyes and fell asleep. I stood over him for several minutes, watching his hands twitch gently on top of the old quilt.

I leaned over and kissed his forehead, carefully avoiding his swollen, discolored little nose.

Chapter Thirteen

THE WICK NEEDED TO BE CHECKED and the kerosene refilled every six hours. I determined to stay awake until midnight to do the first check. Clayton never slept in past six o'clock, so I knew we'd all wake up to do the predawn check.

Mr. Shufelt, Rudy, and I sat in the sitting room listening to the radio and playing cribbage. First there was *Buck Rogers in the 25th Century*. Buck was somewhere in space fighting the forces of evil and darkness.

"That's a sweetheart of a hat, Louise." Mr. Shufelt smiled at me. He had pegged around the cribbage board twice before I had gotten halfway down the first side. "You look like high society."

"It's Ma's," said Rudy.

"I'm just keeping it safe for her till she gets back," I said.

"I'd say that's a fine idea," said Mr. Shufelt. He started to shuffle the cards. "Have another hand?"

"You have a try, Rudy," I said. "I'm finished."

I sat on the other end of the sofa and noticed the edge of a box sticking out from under me. It was Sid's box of shad-dart stuff. Darts are little lures used to catch shad in the spring. I pulled out the box and picked out a small metal disk that had already been painted a bright chartreuse color. I didn't fish much, but I enjoyed making the little lures that Sid, Rudy, and

Dad would use next spring when the shad started running up the river. I found a puff of deer hair and started attaching it to the end of the chartreuse dart.

After Buck Rogers, we listened to *Fibber Magee and Molly*, then *Your Hit Parade*.

"Fifteen ten and a pair's twelve!" said Mr. Shufelt. Rudy tossed his cards on the table.

I felt my eyelids start to droop as the late-night news droned on. I glanced at Rudy next to me on the sofa and saw that he had fallen asleep.

As soon as the radio played "The Star-Spangled Banner," I pushed the shad-dart box back under the sofa and got up to go to the lantern room. Mr. Shufelt was dozing in the wing chair by the window. I left Rudy sleeping on the sofa under Ma's Dresden-plate quilt.

I picked up Dad's flashlight and climbed the winding stairway leading up to the top of the light tower. The flashlight beam on the wall climbed beside me as I walked, lurching and flattening out around the curve of the stairway as I moved.

I stood at the top of the light tower and looked out over the river. Each time the light swung around behind me, my silhouette was cast against the shoreline below, wiggling and yawing across the riverbank like a dark ghost. A barge drifted slowly downriver toward the lighthouse, its flat, boxy outline making a dark rectangle on the water. I wondered who would be traveling down the river this time of night, and whether they were as lonely as I felt at that moment. I saw a black shape standing on the bow: the watchman. He raised an arm in a silent wave as the barge continued downriver past the light.

I had a sudden, aching urge to follow the barge on its journey. To drift down the river past Poughkeepsie, south with the current, past farms and towns all asleep in the darkness. Then silently continue down, down, to drift finally among the tall, metal skyscrapers of New York City. Perhaps the barge would stop there to unload its cargo. But I would continue farther still, now on some other vessel: a sailing ship or a tanker; into Hudson Bay, then Long Island Sound, until I was swept into the swirling current of the Atlantic Ocean.

But Ma wouldn't be there on the vast Atlantic Ocean. I'd still be waiting for her just the same. The waiting was something you couldn't travel far enough to ever get away from. I knew enough to know that what you carry inside is something you can't get away from, no matter how far you travel. I wondered what Ma was carrying inside her that made her want to travel so far away from the lighthouse and the wide, gray Hudson. When she came back, I just might ask her.

Chapter Fourteen

THE LIGHTHOUSE HAD NEVER FELT SO LONELY as during the time that Dad and Sid were gone. Even the early light of day didn't erase the empty feeling in the little rooms. We were up before the morning sun. Mr. Shufelt made us eggs again for breakfast, scrambled this time instead of fried.

"I've got to get the store open, kids," he said. "I'm sure your dad and Sid will be back by tonight." He climbed down the ladder and into his little motorboat. The early-morning mist parted and swirled around the boat as he putt-putted across toward shore. It was just after six o'clock.

The mist burned off an hour later.

"Guess we can put the light out," I said. "It's now officially morning."

We spent the morning cleaning the lighthouse.

"Ought to have it looking nice when Dad and Sid get back," said Rudy. He washed the deck and stood on a ladder to polish the big fog bell that hung halfway up the light tower.

Clayton polished the brass railings and other brightwork in the light tower until it sparkled. I scrubbed the kitchen and swept and dusted the sitting room. I even did the laundry that Sid had left in a pile by the washing machine.

In between all this work, we ran out onto the deck every few minutes to stare at the Hudson City shore, trying to bring our family back by the sheer force of our eyes scanning the riverbank.

The morning day liner went past on her way down to New York City, making an enormous wake that splashed up and over Rudy's clean deck. I put my hand on Rudy's shoulder as we watched the stern of the *Robert Fulton* steaming on down the river.

About noon, we sat down in the kitchen for a lunch of crackers and hard cheese washed down with water from the cistern. Our drinking water was collected in the cellar in a huge concrete-and-metal cistern that was filled with runoff from the roof. A series of metal gutters and pipes came down from the roof and drained into the cistern in the cellar. We were forever shooing seagulls and pigeons from the roof of the lighthouse in an effort to keep our drinking water clean. Before drinking it we mixed powder in the water to take away the slightly musty taste.

After we had finished, I got up from the table. "Back at it, boys! Dad won't recognize the place when he gets back, it'll be so clean!"

"I'm tired of cleaning," said Clayton. He ran his hand gingerly across the bottom of his swollen nose and sniffed. I could see that his hands were dry and red from the brass polish.

I sighed and glanced over at Rudy. His cheeks bulged out at the sides from the load of crackers he had stuffed in there. He shrugged and kept chewing.

"I guess there's no harm in taking an extended lunch break," I said. "Might do us some good to relax."

"Yay!" shouted Clayton. "Telephone! I want to play Telephone!"

"Telephone? But Sid's not here."

"Please, Weezie?"

Rudy drank the last of his water and wiped his mouth on his sleeve. "I can climb up, Weezie—so can you, for Pete's sake."

I was looking at Rudy and then at Clayton, thinking maybe we deserved a little fun. Maybe Telephone was just what we needed. But Ma hated Telephone. She would yell at us from the deck while we were scrambling over the roof and up the sides of the lighthouse.

"You kids get down here!" she'd yell. "Get down here by me!"

"Okaaaayy, Maaaaa," Sid would hoot, his voice echoing along the length of the drainpipe coming out beside Ma's head at the corner of the house. "Weeeee'rrrreee coooommmmmiingg!"

"That's not funny, Sidney!" she'd screech. "You get down here now!" Then in a quieter voice, as she turned to go back inside, but still loud enough for us to hear: "Last thing I want to do is row you across the river with a broken neck."

I glanced out the window at the November sky. "Going to be cold up there on the roof, Rudy."

"I don't care," he said.

"Yeah!" said Clayton. "He don't care!"

"Doesn't care," I corrected.

"I doesn't care, either!" said Clayton. He started jumping up and down. "Telephone! Telephone! Telephone!"

We didn't have a telephone at the lighthouse. We'd seen them in town. There was one at the post office and one in the principal's office at school. My friend Eva Masterman had one in her front hall. I pictured big pipes running underground between houses, echoing words that people spoke and coming out through the black bell-shaped earpieces of the telephones. Of course I knew that telephones ran through wires, but I liked the idea of underground pipes better.

"Ma wouldn't like it," I murmured.

"Well, Ma ain't here, is she?" asked Rudy.

"Isn't here," I muttered.

I pictured Ma rowing across the river from Hudson and the first thing she sees is us on the roof and Clayton on the deck shouting up through the drainpipe playing Telephone. In that same moment, I knew I couldn't stay tiptoeing around forever waiting for Ma to come home. If she did come across the river on this particular afternoon, she'd see that we were still children, still living. There was no way around that fact. We were the Bloom kids, making the best of living on a lighthouse in the middle of the Hudson River. Suddenly I wanted to be up on the roof playing Telephone when Ma came home.

"I'm tired of cleaning this place," I said. "How about you?"

"Let's go!" said Rudy.

Clayton let out a squeal and skipped out through the kitchen door. Rudy and I followed. I grabbed Clayton's coat off the peg by the door on my way out and pulled the door closed behind me with a solid thump.

Telephone is a simple game. All you have to do is shout back and forth through the ends of a drainpipe. The only complicated part was getting to the end of the drainpipe at the roofline. Most of the time, Sid would be the first to climb up the side of the lighthouse to the roof and hoot down through the pipe until Rudy or I got the nerve to climb up, too. Today we'd have to get our courage up without him. Clayton always stayed on the deck and ran from one corner of the house to the other shouting up through the drainpipes as we hollered down.

On deck, Rudy was already halfway up the outside of the lighthouse. He grabbed onto the edges of the granite blocks along the corner and crawled his way upward. Clayton hopped up and down. "Go up, Weezie!"

I looked up at Rudy. "How's the weather up there?"

Rudy swung his knees one at a time up onto the roof ledge and put his face against the gutter to call down to me. His voice came echoing out of the drainpipe in front of us. "Come up, Louise Bloooooooommm. Come up to the rooooooooooofffff!"

"Go up. Go up! Go up!" chanted Clayton. He was still hopping up and down. He pushed my elbow with each "up!"

I nudged his hand away. "Okay, okay."

I pushed Ma's hat tight onto my head, then stepped forward and grabbed the upper edge of the granite block just above my eye level. Pulling with my arms and pushing down with my feet, I followed in Rudy's footsteps up the side of the lighthouse. The November wind blew up my skirt as I got higher, and the chill crept along my backbone.

"Go, Weezie!" I could hear Clayton calling after me.

At the roof ledge, Rudy was squatting and looking out over the river. "No sign of them," he said. "Not anyone."

I nodded and squinted at the shoreline. "They'll be back. Dad won't leave us."

"Like some other people?"

"Hush, Rudy."

I sat and hugged my knees. A seagull swooped and circled then landed on the ridge of the roof behind us. Rudy turned and stood up, leaning against the side of the roof toward the gull. "Shoo!"

The seagull turned one eye toward him and blinked. "Shoo!" said Rudy, louder. He hopped and banged his hands against the side of the roof. The seagull squawked and reluctantly lifted into the air. She swooped back around toward us, looking to see if we might have a crust of bread or a cold potato to toss to her. For a moment the gull was in the air directly in front me. I could see her feet tucked under her snow-white belly and the perfect roundness of her yellow eye. I could hear the air pressing against her long wing feathers. Then her tail tipped and she was gone, gliding and wheeling across the air toward the riverbank.

"Seagulls don't leave their babies until they can fly," said Rudy as he sat back down beside me. "I've seen 'em swimming with their babies in the water and bringing them food."

I was silent.

"They don't leave them until they're ready to be on their own," he said again.

"I know," I said, squinting at the riverbank. I searched the shoreline for Ma. *Let her come home now,* I silently begged the river. *Let her see us on the roof.*

"Seems like people would have as much sense as a seagull," said Rudy.

We stared at the river for a while.

"You ever going to take that hat off?" asked Rudy.

"Maybe," I said. "Maybe not." I turned my head to look at him. "Is that okay?"

He shrugged. "I didn't used to like you wearing it. But I'm kind of used to it now."

"Talk to me!" shouted Clayton from the deck. "Ring, ring! Telephone!"

I leaned over and put my mouth near the downspout. "Helllooooo, Clayton!"

I turned my head so that my ear was against the downspout to listen for his reply. "Helloooo, Weezie!"

Rudy scrambled away toward another corner of the roof. Our job was to make Clayton run from drainpipe to drainpipe answering our shouts.

Rudy hollered down the drainpipe at the opposite roof corner, and Clayton, giggling, went running around the deck. I waited until I heard Clayton's answering hoot up to Rudy, then squatting, maneuvered to the next corner of the roof nearest the light tower. I yelled down through the pipe and was rewarded with the sound of Clayton's footsteps scratching along the deck below. He squealed and banged on the drainpipe. The hollow, tinny echo was followed by his shout. "Testing, ring, ring! Testing, ring, ring!"

"Hello? Who is it?"

"Lighthouse inspector!" boomed Clayton.

"I'm not ready!" I screeched. "Not ready at all. Come back tomorrow!"

"Okaaaaaaaayyyyyy!" Clayton burst into a spasm of giggles. I peered over the edge of the roof ledge and saw him flop to the deck, overcome with the hilarity of it all.

"We don't need an inspection!" I added. "Or dissection, or election, or direction." I paused to think. Clayton was squealing uncontrollably now. I shouted louder down the pipe. "Or a SECTION, or DETECTION, or DEFLECTION!"

"Weezie!" Rudy grabbed me by the shoulder.

I let out a surprised squawk and sat heavily back on the roof to steady myself. "You'll knock me off! Cut it out!"

"Lighthouse inspector's coming!" he hissed in my ear.

I smiled and leaned back over the drainpipe. "Nooooooo inspection todaaaaaay, Bub!" My voice boomed out of the drain.

Clayton stood and hollered up to us. "No inspection today!"

"Weezie!" Rudy grabbed my shoulder again and twisted me around toward the Hudson shore. "The lighthouse inspector's coming!"

I saw a motorboat coming across the river toward us. My first thought was that Ma was finally coming home. In the next second, I saw the dark blue of the man's uniform coat and pants and the U.S. Lighthouse Service hat on top of his head.

My heart lurched in my chest. The inspector from the U.S. Lighthouse Service was coming across the river! There would indeed be an inspection today. And if the lighthouse failed the inspection, Dad could lose his job.

Knees trembling, I climbed down the corner of the house with the bricks tugging at my wool socks like little fingers, and ran inside.

Chapter Fifteen

"GET THE LOGBOOK!" I dumped the remains of lunch in the bucket by the pump and put the plates in the sink.

Rudy got the logbook from its place on the far wall and placed it on the kitchen table.

"Are the beds made?" I glanced around the kitchen and leaned down to blow Clayton's nose.

"Ow!" Clayton flinched. I had forgotten about his tender nose.

"Sorry." I loosened my grip on the handkerchief. "But you and Rudy made the beds, right?"

Clayton nodded. "Yes, Weezie." His voice was muffled by the handkerchief over this nose.

"Did you put away the cleaning bucket you were using on the deck, Rudy?"

"Yes," said Rudy. He turned to go up the stairs to the light tower. "I'm gonna check the lantern room."

"He's almost here!" called Clayton from the front door. He was on tiptoe looking out the four-pane window.

I straightened the quilt on the sofa and looked around the sitting room. The clock tick-tocked in a sharp counterpoint to the thudding of my heart against the side of my throat. What would the inspector say when he found out that Dad wasn't here?

"Clayton."

He walked in from the hallway. "What?"

"If the inspector asks, I'm going to tell him that Dad is in town."

"But he's after Sid."

I knelt down and took Clayton by the shoulders. "I know that, Clayton. I know we're not sure where he is, exactly, but the inspector doesn't need to know that. The only thing he needs to know is that Dad is the best lighthouse keeper on the Hudson River." I stood up and looked over my shoulder toward the river. "So there's no need to tell him about Ma and Sid, and Dad chasing after him. You understand?"

"Yeah, okay." He ran his hand under his nose.

My heart was pounding in my chest and my voice sounded hollow. "I mean it, Clayton. It's really important."

"*Okay, Weezie. I'm not a baby.*"

"Ahoy in the lighthouse!" The inspector's voice boomed from out front.

Clayton looked at me, his eyes big and round. "He's here," he whispered.

Rudy came clumping down the stairs. "He's here!"

I stepped into the hall, my heart making an insistent rhythm against my throat. "I know."

"Ahoy in the lighthouse!" the inspector called again. He probably needed someone to grab the bowline at the dock.

"We could pretend we're not here," murmured Rudy.

"If he came up and found us hiding in here, that'd make things worse," I said. "I guess we better face the music."

I reached for the doorknob. "Man of the house ought to tie up the inspector's boat, Rudy."

He nodded and walked out the door across the deck. Clayton and I stood in the hallway and listened to the clang of the ladder as Rudy climbed down toward the water. My heart counted out the seconds against my throat and I clasped my hands together to keep them from shaking. The lighthouse inspector. Here.

"Remember what I said, Clayton. Dad's in town."

"What's he doing in town?"

"Doesn't matter," I whispered.

"But, Weezie," Clayton persisted. "Is he at Shufelt's? Or at Tomlinson's Hardware?"

"Clayton—"

"I think he's getting the mail!" Clayton smiled. "That's what I'll say."

"Clayton, don't you say anything. You let me do the talking."

He nodded and sniffed. "Okay, Weezie."

There was scuffling on the deck, then Rudy was at the door. He stepped into the hallway and looked around nervously. "Inspector's here."

A tall man appeared behind Rudy. I saw the dark blue uniform and the captain's hat with the word *Inspector* across the front in red letters.

I suddenly remembered I had Ma's hat on. I reached up to grab it from my head, then stepped forward and nodded. "Hello, Inspector." I hoped he didn't hear the uncertainty in my voice.

He touched his hand to the bill of his hat. "Good morning, miss. I'm Inspector Schermerhorn from the Lighthouse Service. Could you tell your father I'm here, please?"

"He's getting the mail!" piped Clayton from beside me.

I bit my lip to keep from scolding Clayton.

"Your mother, then. Mrs. Bloom. She'll be here." The inspector removed his hat and stepped inside the hall.

"No," I said. "She's away."

"Well, then." The inspector looked down at Clayton and raised his eyebrows ever so slightly. "That's quite a bump on the nose you've got there, young man."

"Yes, sir," mumbled Clayton. "Hit it on the works crank."

"He's always getting into trouble of one kind or another," I said quickly. I put my hand on Clayton's head. "He's five."

"Hmmm," murmured the inspector. He wasn't smiling.

My thoughts raced. Was he going to put Clayton's banged nose in his report? Maybe Dad would get in trouble because I had let Clayton near the works crank. I avoided looking at Mr. Schermerhorn. He cleared his throat.

"I'll start the inspection on the deck. Your father can show me the lantern room and logbook when he returns."

"No!" I said, trying not to shout. "You never know how long it'll take Dad . . . in town." I gestured toward Rudy. "Rudy can show you the lantern room." I grabbed Rudy's arm and turned him back up toward the stairs.

"That would be quite unorthodox," said Inspector Schermerhorn. "Very unorthodox." He removed a clipboard from under his arm and a pencil from an inner pocket of his jacket. He wrote something at the top of the clipboard and checked his pocket watch. I strained my neck to see if he had written "unorthodox," but couldn't make anything out. I had the horrifying thought that I might begin to cry if I tried to speak.

Mr. Schermerhorn looked up at Rudy standing on the stairs, then back to me. "I suppose I may as well get started. I can interview your father regarding the logbook upon his return."

I did my best to smile, although my stomach was beginning to feel as though it might leap out of my throat any second.

"We weren't here all night by ourselves, either," said Clayton. "Mr. Shufelt was here. And Ma's coming back soon." He looked up at me. "Right, Weezie?"

"Yes, Clayton. She'll be back soon," I whispered.

Mr. Schermerhorn looked from Clayton to me and back again. "Well," he said. "Well."

I looked at Rudy and motioned with my eyes toward the stairs. He gave a little jump.

"Inspector, sir, would you like to see the lantern room?"

Inspector Schermerhorn gestured to Rudy with his clipboard. "To the lantern room, then, *Mister* Bloom."

Rudy glanced nervously at me before turning to go up the stairs. Inspector Schermerhorn followed behind, holding the clipboard in front of him like a divining rod.

As soon as the inspector's heel disappeared around the curve in the stairs, I grabbed Clayton's hand and pulled him to the kitchen.

"I said no talking!" I hung Ma's hat on a peg with an angry jab.

"Sorry," Clayton mumbled. I saw his lower lip start to tremble.

"Clayton, don't cry. I'm sorry." I steered him toward the sink and motioned toward the slop bucket. "You empty the slop. I'll wash the dishes."

Clayton picked up the bucket by the sink and walked awkwardly out the door, the big metal bucket banging against his knee with every step. He'd dump it in the wooden bin by the door. We mixed our table scraps with ashes from the woodstove all winter long and used the compost in the spring to grow vegetables. Ma was in charge of the vegetable patch and managed to grow enough in the cracks between the rocks of the lower foundation to keep us in fresh greens and vegetables all summer long. I hadn't yet thought to spring and vegetables. Surely Ma would be back by then. I started washing the dishes in the sink.

Clayton came back in, the bucket still banging against his legs, and set it, empty, back on the floor.

I put the last plate on the draining rack and pulled the plug in the sink. "Now we just wait."

A lighthouse inspection usually took several hours. The inspector would check the lantern room to make sure it was well maintained, looking at the lamps, the Fresnel lens, and the wick. He'd check Dad's inventory list and the log carefully to make sure supplies were used economically. He'd check all the brightwork around the lighthouse: the brass railings, fittings, and edgework to make sure it was shiny and smudge free. The lantern works would be wound and run, the fog bell rung. Outside, the condition of the punt, ladder, and derrick would be checked and the deck would be inspected for orderliness and safety. Finally, the logbook entries would be audited and the living quarters inspected for cleanliness and orderliness.

No one really enjoyed an inspection, but Ma used to take it as a personal affront. "If the U.S. Lighthouse Service trusts us to keep boats off the rocks and pull drowning people from the river, they by God ought to trust us to take care of the lighthouse," she'd grouse.

Dad was always calm.

"It's a safety measure, Myra," he'd say.

Ma didn't buy it. "We shouldn't have to put up with it."

"The job requires it," Dad would say.

"I'd like to be able to call my house my own," Ma would say, scowling and crossing her arms across her chest. "Not have someone coming through giving it the white-glove treatment."

"I don't know why you complain," Dad would say. "You keep this house neat as a pin. Never gotten a single write-up. Cleanest lighthouse on the Hudson River, no holds barred. With four kids, too."

"Don't try to appeal to my vanity, Owen," Ma would say, but she'd be smiling a bit now. She'd uncross her arms. "Although it is true that I am a fine housekeeper." She'd stand up and put her hands on Dad's shoulders. "Almost as good a housekeeper as you are lighthouse keeper."

I could see them standing there smiling at each other as I stood in front of the sink looking out the little window onto the river.

"How long we gotta wait, Weezie?" asked Clayton.

I turned and smiled down at him. "Pretty long," I said. "Let's go check the deck before Rudy and the inspector get down from the lantern room."

We went outside and walked around the deck, kicking pebbles off into the water and trying not to touch the railing. I ducked inside the privy and tucked the pile of catalogs into a neat stack. Clayton coiled the rope by the boat derrick.

When we got back inside, the inspector and Rudy were sitting at the kitchen table with the logbook.

"Let's see," said the inspector as he looked at his clipboard.

"Last inspection was April twenty-third of this year. We'll start there." He opened the logbook and began to examine the entries written in Dad's scrawling hand.

We were all so intent on watching Inspector Schermerhorn examine the log that we didn't hear the front door open.

"Daddy!" Clayton squealed. He ran down the hallway.

I turned to look and saw Dad walking toward us and glimpsed Sid as he ducked into the stairway without slowing down. "Dad!"

Dad came into the kitchen, Clayton clinging to his waist. He leaned over and kissed me on the forehead, then put his arm around Rudy. Inspector Schermerhorn stood up and extended his hand. "Mr. Bloom. Inspector Schermerhorn."

Dad shook his hand and smiled. "Yes, sir. I'm sorry I wasn't here to greet you. I assume my children showed you around properly."

"That they did, Mr. Bloom."

"Is Sid okay?" I tried to keep my voice even. How would I sound if they had really just come back from getting the mail? I wondered.

Dad nodded. "He's upstairs, I imagine." He cleared his throat. "Perhaps you'd better say hello while Inspector Schermerhorn and I look at the books."

We didn't need any more persuading than that. The three of us left Dad and Mr. Schermerhorn to the logbook. I grabbed Ma's hat off the peg and put it securely back on my head as I walked up the stairs behind Rudy and Clayton.

Chapter Sixteen

SID WAS LYING ON THE BED, arms under his head and staring at the ceiling. Clayton scooted past me and bounced on the end of the bed. Sid's body moved in a wave with the motion of the bed.

"Hi, Sid!"

I sat on the floor by Sid's head, Rudy perched on the bed at his feet, and Clayton crawled over between Sid and the wall with his knees tucked under his chin.

"This is my room, as I recall," said Sid. "And I don't remember inviting you in."

"We're glad to see you, Sid," I said.

"Yeah," said Rudy. "Real glad."

"What makes you think I'm glad to be back?" asked Sid.

"Didn't you miss us, Sid?" asked Clayton. He snuffled loudly and swallowed.

Sid sighed and turned toward Clayton. "I didn't miss your snotty nose, tell you that much right now." He stopped with his hand reaching out for Clayton's handkerchief. "What happened to you?"

Clayton touched his nose tenderly. The bruise had spread under each eye, making him look like some kind of pale and hairless raccoon. "Weezie hit me with the crank handle."

Sid twisted his neck and looked at me.

"It was an accident!"

"I leave for one night and things fall apart, is that the way it is?" asked Sid.

"Guess so," I murmured.

"Don't leave again," said Rudy.

"I ain't promising anything," said Sid. He tucked his hands back behind his head. "Guess you'll just have to treat me real nice and maybe I'll stay."

"That's not funny, Sid," I said.

"Was I joking?"

I reached out and touched Sid's elbow. "What if you're gone when Ma gets home? How would that make her feel?"

"What if you're wearing her hat when she gets back?" said Sid. "How would *that* make her feel?"

"Yeah, it's Ma's hat," said Clayton.

"I'm just keeping it safe," I said. I ran my palm over the petals on the front. "Besides, it makes me feel—"

"What?" said Sid.

"I don't know. Protected."

"Protected," repeated Sid. "Pink straw's not going to protect you from much." He touched the hat brim with a forefinger. "Guess it's your business if you want to look screwy."

The thing is, it wouldn't matter what Sid or Clayton or Rudy said. I was going to wear the hat. It made me feel the opposite of screwy. It made me feel snug and secure, somehow. Calmer. Like I could wait it out until Ma came back, no matter how long that might be. It was still Ma's hat, I knew that, and I'd give it back gladly when she got home.

"I made something for you." I thrust my hand out toward Sid.

Sid turned and looked at the deer-hair shad dart pinched between my thumb and finger.

"Huh." He held the dart in front of his face and twirled it so he could look at it from all sides. "Pretty one." He hooked the dart to his shirtfront and lay back down. A single word came out in a low mumble when he spoke. "Thanks."

We sat quietly then. I could hear Dad and the inspector talking downstairs in the kitchen.

It was Rudy who finally spoke. "Did you see any sign of Ma?" he asked quietly. "Anyone seen her?"

From the side, I watched Sid's mouth move as he spoke to the ceiling, his lips parting and coming together to form the words. "No. No sign of her." He rolled over on his side and gave Clayton a push with his hand. "Now get out of here. I'm tired."

Chapter Seventeen

AFTER SID CAME BACK, the cold came down from Canada, and the river began to freeze. The ice was only thin, floating patches here and there by Thanksgiving, so Dad rowed across the river to the Athens side and brought back a turkey from the Peter Farm. Mr. Peter had chopped the head off and drained it for him. By the time it got to us, the bird was a round headless bundle of feathers tucked under Dad's arm, with the feet sticking out below like two gnarled hands.

I had a big pot of water boiling on the stove all ready for the plucking. Sid and I carried the pot between us out to the deck. Sid grabbed the turkey by the feet and dunked it in the boiling water, the steam swirling up and around the carcass and into our faces like the mist from a witch's cauldron. It reminded me of the three witches in a play we had been reading in school.

"Double, double, toil and trouble!" I shrieked. "Fire burn and cauldron bubble!"

Sid lifted the turkey out of the pot and held it at arm's length, dripping, toward us. Rudy grabbed at the dripping turkey. A handful of feathers came off in his grip. Clayton reached out and plucked a handful and threw them sideways off the deck. We pulled and plucked until the feathers wouldn't come easily and

Sid dunked the mottled carcass in the water again to loosen them. Feathers drifted up and out over the river, falling to the gray water below, or onto the rocks, where the cold November wind pushed them into the cracks between the rocks like autumn leaves.

"Save some of those downy ones," said Sid, stuffing a handful of small feathers in his jacket pocket. He was thinking about fishing, again.

Our fingers got red with the cold as the wind blew across the deck. The water lost its heat. Sid handed me the turkey, and he and Rudy went back inside to get the second pot of hot water. Clayton followed behind, wiping his nose on his mitten.

Last Thanksgiving, it was Ma who held the turkey while we all pulled at the feathers.

"Look at that, all my little chickens plucking a turkey!" she had said. "Clayton, put some effort into it; you're falling behind."

It had started to snow as we were all out there on the deck, the turkey bobbing this way and that as we pulled the feathers from its pale pink skin. Ma had started gobbling like a turkey, and I looked up at her. The tiny flakes of that winter's first snow drifted down and landed on her dark hair and the shoulders of her coat. She smiled at me, and I saw a single snowflake, delicate and perfect as a teardrop from God, resting on the lashes of her left eye.

I had been singing—a hymn, maybe "Simple Gifts"—while the feathers floated around us.

"You've got a song for everything," said Rudy. I remember thinking that there was most certainly a song for everything.

Ma collected some of the soggy feathers and dried them by the stove. Later that winter, when we were stranded in the lighthouse, we snipped the ends of the feathers to make quill pens and dipped them in bottles of Dad's fountain-pen ink.

Standing there on the deck with Ma gone and me holding the turkey in her place, I felt an ache inside me rolling and sloshing like dirty water in a bucket. I was mad at Ma for leaving, and sad that my brothers and I weren't enough to make her stay. It was a fight inside me between the anger and sadness to see which one would win. I knew if I didn't get my mind on something else, my grief would roil up to the surface and explode out of me like thundering plates of broken river ice heaved up against the shore. And there was no song that would make me feel better. No song that I wanted to sing, anyway.

My arms were starting to ache with the effort of holding up the fifteen-pound bird.

"Where's that hot water?" I yelled. No answer from the inside of the lighthouse.

Still holding the turkey at arm's length, I banged against the door with my shoulder.

"Where's the hot water?" I yelled again. "Sid! Rudy!"

Sid opened the door and I stumbled into the kitchen. "Don't get your shorts in a knot, Louise," he said. "We're coming."

I glanced around the kitchen. Rudy and Clayton were sitting at the table eating cookies that I had made the day before. Sid put the last piece of his own cookie in his mouth and grinned.

"Just taking a short break," he said, and wiped his mouth with the back of his hand. "Pretty good cookies."

"I was out there waiting!" I said. "How long were you boys

going to make me stand out there in the cold, holding this drip-ping wet, half-plucked *turkey*?" My voice rose and squeaked on the last word.

"For pity's sake, Louise," said Sid. "What's the matter with you?"

"We didn't mean to make you mad, Weezie," said Rudy. He held up a half-eaten cookie. "You want one?"

Clayton snuffled and looked from me to Sid. Suddenly the sight of them all made me sick. I couldn't believe that they were related to me.

"No, I do not want a cookie," I said. I swung the turkey up over the edge of the counter. It landed with a hollow, squishy thud on the bottom of the sink. I turned and faced my brothers.

"You don't get it, do you?" I said. "You come in here and just forget about me out there with the turkey! It's no wonder Ma left!" I turned and stomped out of the kitchen, leaving them with the cookies and the half-plucked turkey.

Chapter Eighteen

ON THANKSGIVING MORNING, I woke up as soon as I heard Dad clumping down the metal stairs from the light tower. I got dressed and put Ma's hat on and went downstairs. I stoked the fire in the coal stove and went outside to get the turkey. I checked the thermometer on the stove. I would have to keep the oven as close to a steady 325 degrees as possible all morning.

Last year, I had helped Ma with Thanksgiving dinner. I'd spread melted butter on the rolls before they went into the oven and mashed the potatoes.

We hummed "Ain't We Got Fun" while Ma taught me how to roll out pastry to make a pie. I sighed, remembering. How could someone seem so happy on the outside and be so unhappy on the inside? That's another thing I would ask Ma if I ever saw her again.

I put the turkey in its roasting pan on the table and started to jam wet handfuls of celery and crackers into the cavity.

Clayton and Rudy tromped into the kitchen. "I'm hungry!" said Clayton.

I fluttered my hands, gooey with wet crackers, over the top of the turkey. "I'm stuffing the bird. Get the Ralston out of the pantry."

Sid joined the two younger boys at the table to eat cereal. He waved his spoon at the pale turkey. "Don't ruin the turkey, Louise. I'm looking forward to it."

Clayton wrinkled his nose as he watched me. "That doesn't look like Ma's stuffing."

"It looks different after it's cooked," I said.

"Hope so," said Rudy. "Or we're in trouble."

"I'm trying to make a meal here!" I said, my voice rising. "And I don't see any of you offering to help."

"Sooooorry," said Sid. He rolled his eyes at Rudy and Clayton. "Louise is touchy this morning, boys. Better leave her alone."

"That sounds like a wonderful idea," I said, jamming the last handful of stuffing into the bird so hard it rattled the pan.

After the turkey was safely in the oven and I had eaten breakfast, I went downstairs and got the sack of potatoes from the basement.

"What can I do to help?" asked Dad. He was waiting at the top of the stairs when I emerged with the sack of potatoes.

"Well, I'm starting the potatoes. Then I've got squash to peel, johnnycake and mincemeat pie to make. I've got to start the cranberry sauce, and gravy I'll make at the very last."

"Louise, we don't need all that," said Dad, taking the sack from me and plunking it down by the sink. "Turkey and potatoes with stuffing would be fine. I'll peel potatoes and we'll eat the cookies that you made the other day for dessert. You're biting off more than you can chew, here."

"If you didn't want to help, why did you ask?" I clamped my mouth shut in a thin line, but the words had already come out.

"Careful how you speak to me, Louise," said Dad.

"Sorry, Dad." I looked up at him. "But I'm making a real Thanksgiving dinner no matter who helps."

Dad sighed. "Why are you taking this on, Weezie?"

I brushed past him, my heart suddenly fluttering, and started taking potatoes out of the sack. "Because it's Thanksgiving. And that's what we always have at Thanksgiving: turkey, stuffing, potatoes, squash, johnnycake, cranberry sauce, gravy, mincemeat pie, and peas. So that's what we're having!" *And because it will bring Ma back,* I added silently.

Dad looked past me out the window over the sink and said nothing. I don't know what he saw out there, but after a few seconds, he gave a sigh and turned to me.

"All right," said Dad. "Then you're going to need help." He picked up two enormous butternut squash from the floor by the sink.

"Rudy! Sid!" He called to the ceiling.

The boys came clumping down the stairs and into the kitchen.

Dad, still holding the squash, nodded toward me. "Weezie needs some help getting this meal on the table. You two boys start peeling potatoes."

"Aw, Dad—" began Rudy.

"I don't want to hear it," said Dad. "Start peeling."

"What about me?" said Clayton, who had come downstairs behind the other two.

Dad hefted the squash. "You and I have some squash to smash. Come on."

They went outside on the deck to smash the squash into manageable-size pieces for peeling.

"When's dinner?" said Sid. He grabbed a knife and a potato and sat down at the kitchen table.

"I'm planning on two o'clock," I said. "It'll be later if you don't get going on those potatoes."

"La-di-da, Miss Louise," said Sid. "Don't worry, we'll get 'em peeled by two o'clock."

"I'm hungry," said Rudy.

"Now that you mention it . . ." said Sid. He put his knife down on the table and squatted in front of the icebox.

I grabbed a can of peas from the pantry. "For pity's sake, you just had breakfast."

"That was hours ago," said Rudy.

I glanced at the clock and was horrified to see that Rudy was right. It was nearly noon and I hadn't even started the johnny-cake or the pie. Never mind cranberry sauce and gravy.

Sid stood up from the icebox with a lump of cheese in his hand. "This'll hit the spot."

"Hey, let me have some of that," said Rudy. He lunged toward Sid.

"No sirree, Bobby." Sid twisted away. They started chasing each other around the table.

As usual, they were like wolf puppies, yipping and nipping at each other, running around the table in an endless game of chase. Rudy and Sid were forever trying to sumo-wrestle. Placing their hands on each other's shoulders, they'd push and strain against each other until one of them was forced to step backward and concede. Dad sometimes joined in, threatening with a laugh to "knock one of you boys into the middle of next week." Now they began to wrestle for the cheese.

"Peel the potatoes!"

They ignored me.

While they tussled, I got cornmeal out of the pantry and read the corn-bread recipe off the box, mentally calculating a schedule to make the rest of the meal. If I made the johnnycake now, I could make the pie later and let it bake while we ate. I'd worry about cranberry sauce and gravy later.

Cornmeal, flour, eggs, and milk. I dumped ingredients into a big crockery bowl and began to stir with one of Ma's big wooden spoons until I realized I had forgotten to put baking powder in.

I left the bowl on the edge of the sink and went in search of baking powder. I found the can on the shelf. When I took the top off the can, there was no baking powder inside. A wad of what looked like folded cardboard was stuffed in the can.

Rudy had been cutting the box tops off Ralston cereal boxes for the last few months. He was saving up for a Tom Mix Junior Deputy Kit.

"There's a badge and Tom Mix spurs!" he had said, reading the back of the cereal box.

"Well, you'd better find a safe place to save those box tops. I'm not keeping track of them," I had said.

Apparently the baking-powder can had looked like a safe place to Rudy.

"Rudy!" I said as I walked back into the kitchen.

"Huh?" said Rudy. He was straining against Sid's shoulders as they tried to push each other backward. The cheese, still gripped in Sid's hand, was a misshapen blob against Rudy's shirt.

"Did you dump the baking powder?" I held up the baking-powder can.

"What?"

"Never mind."

I turned my back and leaned against the sink. I heard grunting and the scrape of shoes against the floor, and I was suddenly pushed against the sink.

"Sorry!" said Sid and Rudy almost simultaneously.

"You're supposed to be peeling potatoes!" I yelled.

I whirled around and my elbow hit the bowl on the sideboard, sending it crashing to the floor. The pottery cracked in a neat line, producing two perfect melon-shaped halves. The coarse, gooey cornmeal batter splattered in a swath across the floor. The spoon clacked along the floorboards and came to rest under the icebox.

"Damn it!" the curse burst out of me in a shriek. I threw the baking-powder can onto the floor. I pressed my lips shut to keep from swearing anymore and stood staring at the mess.

"What happened?" Dad and Clayton were back inside, armfuls of chunks of squash cradled against their shirts.

I was horrified to feel my lower lip begin to tremble. I clamped them together even harder and simply waved my hand at the mess on the floor. I didn't dare look any of them in the eye for fear I'd burst into tears.

"Was that our johnnycake?" asked Clayton.

"My box tops!" said Rudy. He bent over and picked up the can.

"Nice going," said Sid with a laugh.

"Yuck," said Clayton, looking at the cornmeal goo on the floor.

"They're horsing around when they should be helping!" I

shrieked. "They haven't peeled one potato! And now I can't make johnnycake because there's no baking powder!"

"Oh, for crying out loud," said Sid. "I'll clean this up." He stomped over to the mess and picked up the two halves of the bowl. "Clayton, you get me the mop." He waved the pieces of the bowl in the air.

"The baking powder's in the sugar bowl," said Rudy. "I dumped it in there."

Sid tossed the broken bowl into the slop bucket. "Rudy, get a new bowl and the cornmeal and start another batch. Tell us what you have left to do, Louise, and we'll do it together. Just stop crying, for pity's sake."

"That sounds like a great plan," said Dad. Stepping over the cornmeal, he let the squash fall into the sink.

"No more slouching around, boys," he said. "We're all working together on this."

"Yes, Dad," mumbled Rudy. "Sorry, Weezie."

Together, we managed to get Thanksgiving on the table and sat down to eat around four o'clock. The potatoes and squash were kind of cold by the time the corn bread came out of the oven, but the turkey was just right.

We all held hands around the table, and Dad said grace. He thanked God for a lot of things: turkey and johnnycake and a family working together to get dinner on the table. He thanked God for the lighthouse and a good job and for letting us wake up every day to the sighing sound of the Hudson River. And at the end, he thanked God for Myra, who gave him the four beautiful children sitting around this table.

I looked at the door, expecting Ma to arrive any minute.

She still had time to come in and sit down to dinner with us. How could she stay away? Surely this great, aching want of mine must keep her up at night, knocking against her windows and haunting the chilly corners of her bedroom. Couldn't she feel my wanting her reaching out across the hills and highways to wherever she was right at this very moment?

"You expecting someone?" said Dad.

I shrugged and scooped up a forkful of cold mashed potatoes. "No," I said. "No one."

But I watched the door all through dinner and then dessert, hoping Ma would walk in to sit down and taste the pie made from mincemeat she herself had canned last fall.

She never showed. After the last dishes were washed and the floor was swept, she was still just as gone as she had been that day in October when we got home from school.

No more the scarlet maples flash and burn
Their beacon-fires from hilltop and from plain;
The meadow-grasses and the woodland fern
In the bleak woods lie withered once again.

The trees stand bare, and bare each stony scar
Upon the cliffs; half frozen glide the rills;
The steel-blue river like a scimitar
Lies cold and curved between the dusky hills.
—CHRISTOPHER CRANCH, "December"

Chapter Nineteen

SID AND I STOOD OUTSIDE the Hudson post office, shift-ing from foot to foot trying to stay warm. It was a Friday, the first week of December. We stopped at the post office every Friday on the way home from school. Rudy had gone in to get the mail while we waited. Mrs. Baskin, the postmistress, certainly could talk. And since Ma had been gone, it seemed that our sad plight was her favorite topic of conversation. "Heard anything from your ma?" she'd ask. Of course she would know if we had heard anything, being the postmistress. "It's such a shame." She'd sigh and shake her head as she handed us the mail. "Such a shame." We took to sending just one of us in, and the rest waited outside. The person inside could always say they had a brother or sister waiting and have an excuse to leave quickly.

Rudy had been inside for at least ten minutes, and we were beginning to despair of him getting away.

"Guess I better go in and rescue him," said Sid. He started up toward the post office when Rudy burst out of the door.

"There's letters from Ma!" shouted Rudy. He ran across the porch and down to the street, waving a fistful of mail over his head. "One for each of us!" He skidded to a stop in front of us.

Rudy handed Sid and me each a letter. I turned mine over.

There was no return address, but the writing was unmistakably Ma's. *Miss Louise Bloom, General Delivery, Hudson, New York.*

My heart skipped a beat. "It looks like a card," I said.

"Yes, sir!" said Rudy. "Christmas card I bet!"

Sid was silent as he turned the envelope addressed to him over in his hands.

I looked at the postmark printed across the three-cent stamp—Sacramento, California.

"Can't get any farther away than that," muttered Sid. He'd been looking at the postmark on his card as well.

"Doesn't matter, Sid," I said. "She sent cards!"

Sid grunted.

"Maybe . . . maybe. What do you think it means?" spluttered Rudy.

"She's coming home for Christmas!" I squealed. My feet crunched on the snow as I jumped from foot to foot, this time from excitement, the cold forgotten. "Don't you see? She's coming back—that's our Christmas gift. And she's writing to let us know!"

Rudy grinned and stared at his envelope. We stood in a cluster outside the post office imagining Ma's wonderful homecoming. I could see the decorated tree, hear the laughter, and see Ma sitting where she loved to sit most of all—in the wing chair by the sitting-room window.

A surge of joy came up from my frozen feet and ran right up my body and out of my mouth. I started singing:

"We'll all run out to meet her when she comes.
Oh, we'll all run out to meet her when she comes!"

I hooked my arm through Rudy's for a do-si-do, and we began skipping in a circle, shouting at the top of our lungs.

"We'll all have chicken and dumplings when she comes.
Oh, we'll all have chicken and dumplings when she comes!"

I unhooked with Rudy and reached out to link arms with Sid, but he pulled away. I stopped skipping and looked up at him, expecting him to sing, but the look on his face silenced me.

"You chumps," said Sid. He spit in the snow. "Ma's gone for good. The sooner you get that through your thick heads, the better."

Rudy and I looked at him, too stricken to speak.

"But, Sid—" I began.

"But nothing," he said. "Let's go."

Sid turned and tossed his unopened envelope from Ma onto the ground, then started walking toward the river.

"We'll see who's right when we open these cards!" I called after him.

"Yeah, we'll see!" echoed Rudy.

We took off after Sid. I stooped to pick Sid's envelope out of the snow and tucked it into my coat pocket.

When we came out of the line of trees next to the river, we were breathless from running. Dad and Clayton were standing by the river waiting for us. The river was frozen solid. I could see the punt hanging on its derrick and the rounded shape of our extra rowboat upside down on the lighthouse deck. Sid was already walking across the ice to the lighthouse.

"We got letters from Ma!" said Rudy, holding up his envelope for Dad to see.

Dad took the envelope from Rudy and looked at it, then handed it back. "Looks like it," he said. "I'll be damned."

I handed the rest of the mail—four letters and another card—to Dad.

"Did I get one?" asked Clayton.

Dad took the card off the pile and handed it to Clayton. "This one has your name on it, son," he said. Dad quickly looked through the rest of the envelopes.

I suddenly realized what he was looking for.

"Yours must have gotten delayed," I said. "Or put in the wrong mailbox. I'll go back and ask Mrs. Baskin." I turned and started to sprint for the post office.

"No, Louise!" said Dad. I stopped and turned back toward Dad.

"No need," he said. "That's nice you kids got letters." He motioned to me with the packet of letters. His brown mitten looked coarse and dirty against the white of the envelopes. "Come on, now. Let's get home."

When we got back to the lighthouse, I ran upstairs to my room and shut the door. I wanted to open Ma's card in private. I sat on the edge of my bed and ran a shaking finger under the flap to open the envelope.

It *was* a Christmas card. On the front was a snowy winter scene of a pine tree with a yellow star above. A red cardinal was perched in the tree—a bright spot against the dark green branches. Sparkles of glitter were sprinkled over the snow and the branches of the tree.

I tilted the card in my hands and watched the sparkles glint and wink at me. Ma had sent a card! I stared at the glittered pine tree, imagining the handwritten message of love, remembrance, and hope that she had undoubtedly written. *Can't wait to see you,* the message would say. *I'll be home on Christmas Eve. Sorry I've been away, but I'll explain when I return. And I'll never leave you again.* Another surge of joy welled up inside me, and I hugged the card to my chest. Then, with trembling fingers, I lifted it open.

Inside, I read the preprinted message SEASON'S GREETINGS. Below that, in Ma's tidy script, were the words *Love, Ma.* That was it. Just enough love for two handwritten words.

My mouth dry, heart racing, I turned the card over. There was nothing on the back except the words WARNER CARD COMPANY, WEAVERVILLE, CALIF. in tiny print at the bottom. A dull ache began to grab at my stomach.

I stared at the words *Love, Ma* and tried to imagine my mother writing them. I saw her grasping the pen like I'd seen her do so many times at the kitchen table while she was writing letters or putting labels on jelly jars. I imagined Ma's face as she wrote the word *love,* but I couldn't tell if she was smiling.

I followed her as she walked to the post office in Sacramento, California, and I saw her putting the cards, one each for me, Sid, Rudy, and Clayton, in the slot.

And at the moment, in my mind's eye, that those cards passed through the slot, I knew Ma wasn't coming back to the lighthouse. Not for Christmas. Not ever.

A wave of horrible, aching anger moved through me. Why did Ma have me if she was just going to leave me? Why did she marry Dad and have four kids if she wasn't going to stay? I grabbed the envelope from the bed and ran downstairs and out onto the deck. My breath came out in ragged clouds in the cold air as I stood by the railing. I dropped the card and envelope on the deck and ground them into the stone with my shoe. I stomped until my thighs ached and the paper of the card and envelope were streaked with dirty brown and gray.

Holes appeared in the pine tree and erased the cardinal. Bits of glitter stuck to the toes of my shoes. I kicked violently at a mound of snow at the base of one of the rail posts to get the glitter off. I kept kicking even after the snow had been knocked away and I was simply hitting the post.

When I couldn't kick anymore, I picked up the ruined card and stood at the railing and ripped it into pieces. The ragged, dirty bits of paper fluttered down onto the river, where they were soon lost on the rough, gray surface of the ice.

Chapter Twenty

THE NEW YEAR, 1939, DAWNED COLD AND BLEAK.
Each morning we walked to school across the ice, following
spots of tobacco juice that Dad had spit out to mark a safe trail.
Miss Kazmaier had finally given up trying to get me to be in the
Glee Club. Even though I knew I didn't want to rejoin, part of
me was sad that she no longer mentioned it.

In mid-January, there was a warm spell, and the river became
our jailer. The melting, moving ice made travel to shore impossible. We lived on potatoes, crackers, and canned milk during
the deepest part of the winter.

Looking out from the lighthouse, I saw only cold, gray sky
merging with the cold, gray earth—the skeletal arms of the shoreline trees the only indication where one stopped and the other
began. The river had heaved great sheets of ice against the riverbank like a restless sleeper impatient for morning throwing off
the bedclothes with a long, chilly arm. The river made its presence known with a growling moan deep beneath the ice that I
could hear through the kitchen floor.

Even ice fishing was made impossible by the jagged and
uneven edges of the great ice sheets stacked upon one another.
There was no need to light the lamps in the light tower because
there was no river traffic. The day liners and great barges

wouldn't resume their daily travels up and down the river until the ice had cleared away in the spring.

One cold night in February, a loud rumbling woke me in my bed. I lay there, stiff and staring into the darkness as the lighthouse shuddered around me. Several bangs and thuds came from the kitchen below me, as ice heaved against the lighthouse foundation.

"Dad!" I heard Clayton call from his room.

The shuddering stopped and the lighthouse was silent.

I got out of bed and wrapped the quilt around me as I walked into the hallway. Sid, Rudy, and Clayton were clustered together near the stairway. The smell of coal smoke met me as I stepped up behind them.

"Dad?" Rudy called down the stairway. "Dad? You okay?"

"Yah," came the reply from downstairs. "Ice hit us." There was a thumping and the sound of metal scraping against something. "Sid and Rudy, get down here. I need your help."

We all trooped down the stairs to the kitchen. The smell of coal smoke was stronger in the kitchen and the air was thick and dark. The kerosene lantern over the kitchen table was still swaying slightly, causing shadows to crawl around the objects in the room.

The stovepipe had been knocked out of the chimney, and a gentle plume of smoke from the night fire was wafting out of the free end of the pipe. Dad was struggling to fit the pipe back into the opening in the wall.

"Damn it." Dad coughed as he leaned across the stove, grasping the stovepipe. The pipe jerked with Dad's hand against it, and bits of ash and soot sprinkled down the wall behind the stove. "Sidney—see if you can get around back of the stove."

Sid moved to the side of the stove and tried to squeeze behind to get within easy arm's reach of the stovepipe.

He was too big.

"I can do it!" said Clayton.

Dad turned to Clayton. "I'm afraid you're not tall enough. Couldn't reach the pipe."

"Let him try, Dad," said Rudy. "He can stand on the soapstone."

Dad considered it for a second or two. "Guess it might work. Come on up here, Clayton."

"What a minute," I said. "Put on my slippers and a pair of mittens."

Clayton stood on the soapstone and reached toward the top of the stovepipe. He grasped the pipe in his little mittened hands and gently guided it back into the hole in the wall.

"Good job, Clayton!" said Rudy.

Dad grabbed Clayton off the stove and tossed him in the air. "That's my Right-Hand Man."

Clayton grinned and laughed as Dad caught him and swung him down to the floor.

"If it gets below zero tomorrow, I'm going into town," said Dad. He was slightly out of breath from tossing Clayton. "I've 'bout had it with canned milk and crackers."

We were silent. Although we all desperately wanted the fresh milk and vegetables that a trip to town would provide, we didn't want Dad walking across the ice.

"What's with the long faces?" said Dad. "Almanac says we're due for a cold spell. I won't go unless it's cold enough."

I woke the next morning to pale sunlight. My nose was cold.

I watched my breath puff out in a small, moist cloud and pressed my hands tightly against my neck to keep the cold from seeping into the warm cocoon of my blanket. I could hear someone downstairs in the kitchen clanking away at the cookstove. Dad was probably stoking up the morning fire.

I gathered my courage, jumped out of bed, and grabbed my dress off the back of the chair. I dove back under the covers, carrying a great swath of cold air that sent shivers up my spine as I lay flat and waited for my body to warm the bed once again. I wriggled out of my nightgown and into my dress, then hopped out and grabbed Ma's hat and my stockings from the chair. I scurried on tiptoes downstairs to the kitchen. The coal stove was already sending out welcome waves of dry heat that greeted me as I entered the kitchen.

It wasn't Dad sitting on his haunches in front of the stove door, though. It was Sid. I pulled a kitchen chair close to the stove and sat down to pull on my stockings.

"Where's Dad?"

Sid turned his head slightly and glanced at me from the corner of his eye. "Went into town."

I glanced at the clock over the kitchen sink. Not quite seven. "The ice?"

Sid stood up and fit the curved handle he had been poking the fire with back into one of the round stovetop lids. "Nobody knows the river ice better'n Dad. He'll be fine."

I heard footsteps overhead and knew the two younger boys were up. "Right," I said. "He wouldn't go if it wasn't safe." I stood up and walked to the wall by the door and stuck my feet into a pair of Dad's old moccasins. "Guess I better get breakfast going."

We had oatmeal with canned milk and a little brown sugar. I remembered the day that Rudy had cried because the kids at school had made fun of him because he didn't know that milk came from cows. He was in first grade. Thought milk came from a can. Your vision of life is a little different looking out from the lighthouse.

After breakfast, I cleaned up the kitchen and sent the boys upstairs to make the beds. I looked at the calendar on the kitchen wall—Tuesday. Guess we'd be going to school tomorrow if Dad decided the ice was firm.

I walked upstairs to get a book. Rudy and Clayton were playing in their room.

The book was on my dresser—*Swallows and Amazons*. I had taken it out of the library before the thaw in the river ice, along with several others: *The Incredible Adventures of Dr. Branestawm* (which I had finished) and *The Hobbit: Or There and Back Again* (which I hadn't yet started). We all did a lot of reading in the winter, often going to the library twice a week when the river ice permitted.

I took the book down to the sitting room and started to read. I was content for an hour or more to wander with Swallow on her adventures. Not wanting to bend the pages of a library book, or to walk upstairs to retrieve the marker I had in my room, I looked about for a bookmark.

There is a large sideboard in our sitting room that holds the table linen and fancy silverware. Our large mantel clock sits atop it. The top drawer of the sideboard is a kind of catchall. I suppose every house has a drawer like it: a place to tuck odds and ends too good to throw away, but that otherwise would clutter up the shelves and tabletops. In addition to bits of string, old marbles, thumbtacks, cans of shoe polish, and broken lead soldiers, our drawer also held a stack of old envelopes that Dad saved to use for scratch paper. I opened the drawer and riffled through the envelopes, hoping to find a slender one to use as a bookmark.

I noticed the edge of a photograph sticking out from under an envelope and pulled it out. I lifted up the photograph and stood there by the sideboard, drawer still open. It was an old photo of Ma and Dad with me as a newborn and Sid. Sid was standing in between my parents, and Dad was holding me in his arms. I remembered the photograph, had seen it many times, but now it seemed to take on a new significance. I looked at Ma standing there, looking forward, but not toward the camera. Her eyes were focused on something just to the side, beyond the camera and beyond my seeking gaze. I stared at her face and willed the young, smooth-faced woman in the photograph to turn her head toward me. Now, as I looked at the picture, it seemed obvious that Ma was going to leave someday in the future: I could see it written on her face. *Twenty-twenty hindsight* is what Dad calls it—being able to look back and see things laid out in perfect, obvious fashion.

I sure had perfect vision now, looking at Ma's face in that photo. It made my eyes ache. Her leaving was shouted in her shadowed eyes, her tilted head, her empty arms. Because it was Dad who was holding the newborn that had been me. I flipped the photo over. *June 15, 1925,* was scrawled across the back. I had been three days old when the picture was taken. I looked at my own small face surrounded by bonnet and blanket. Was I still Louise Elizabeth then, at the tender age of three days, or had I already become Weezie? And what about Sid? I looked at him there between my parents, already standing by himself with no one to hold his hand. I suppose it was no real wonder that he was angry all the time.

I heard one of the boys on the stairs and suddenly felt foolish standing there trying to read a photograph like tea leaves. It would be better as a bookmark. I tucked the picture between the pages of *Swallows and Amazons* and shut the book with a snap.

"Hallo in the lighthouse!" came a call from outside.

"Dad's back!" shouted Clayton as he and Rudy came tromping down the stairs.

We all ran outside onto the deck. Dad was on the ice, pulling a sled loaded with boxes of groceries. "Anybody home?!" he shouted.

"Nobody here but us chickens!" yelled Rudy.

"Well, come help me lug this up, you chickens."

Dad had bought it all: cabbage, turnips, squash, and carrots; three quarts of fresh milk; eggs, butter, and cheese; and meat. In the bottom of a box that Sid carried in, there were four oranges and a bag of horehound candy.

"I want an orange!" said Clayton. "Can I eat an orange, Dad?"

Dad smiled. "That's what oranges are for, boy."

Clayton squealed and took an orange.

Dad reached into the box. "And I think I'll have a piece of this here candy," he said. "How about you, Sid?" He reached in the striped bag and held out a piece.

Sid grinned. "Absolutely."

Dad passed out candy to us. "You, too, Clayton. You'll have to eat that orange later. We've got candy to take care of, here."

We all stood around the table grinning at each other sucking on the sweet, musky horehound candy.

"This is good," murmured Rudy.

I looked at Dad standing there with the bag of candy still in one hand as he rolled the piece of candy around in his mouth. I thought of him holding me as an infant in that picture and knew he'd never leave us. He wasn't going to go off looking for whatever there was to find somewhere else. He was our father and he'd always be here to keep the light lit for us. No matter what.

"L-O-double L-I-P-O-P spells lollipop!" sang Rudy.

"Lollipop song!" shouted Clayton.

Rudy started again, and Clayton and I joined in, shouting at the end of each line, while Sid and Dad unpacked the rest of the groceries.

"L-O-double L-I-P-O-P spells lollipop, lollipop.
That's the only decent kind of CANDY!"

When we got to the end, Dad and Sid joined in the shouting on the "FOR ME!" Then we all stood smiling around the table.

"This is good," I said. And it was.

Chapter Twenty-one

EVER SINCE DAD'S TRIP INTO TOWN, we'd been walking to school across the ice. Dad would get up early and walk to shore, spitting tobacco juice as he went so that we had a path to follow safely to shore.

On Valentine's Day, Clayton fussed about not being able to come to school with us.

"You'll be coming with us next year, Clayton," I said. "First grade."

"I want to come now."

"Well, you can't, squirt," said Sid. "Hell, I wish I could stay home with you."

"I'll do the swearing around here," came Dad's voice from the kitchen.

"Sorry, Dad," said Sid.

"You'll be late," called Dad. "Clayton, I need my Right-Hand Man in here. Don't be jawing with them, we've got work to do today."

Clayton's face brightened. He turned and went to the kitchen without a look back.

I went outside to wait for Sid and Rudy. Ma's straw hat didn't do much to block the wind blowing across the river, but I wore it instead of a warmer wool cap. Down on the ice, I leaned forward on my knees and brushed away an arm's length of snow. Up close, the river ice was clear on top and dark gray underneath. There were air bubbles, hollow and brittle, trapped in the ice. I saw bits of leaf and other debris: a small stick, an acorn cap. A sprig of fir branch was trapped near the top of the ice. I rubbed my mitten over it.

Getting up, I ran and then slid along the ice. The smooth soles of my boots moved noiselessly along the slick surface. The river whispered to me in its rumbling winter voice as I skated in circles. I watched the toes of my boots make long, swooping tracks as the snow flew out from my feet. I could feel the cold against my cheeks and the ice beneath my feet and a calm, quiet gladness in my heart that I was here on the river with the pale winter sun. I hummed, making a tuneless rippling in the back of my throat in time to my feet.

Sid and Rudy banged out the door and down the ladder. I skated over to join them as they stepped onto the ice. The wind was blowing down the river from Coxsackie. A kind of gusting, halfhearted wind that hinted of the March thaw that would trap us back in the lighthouse for a time.

Sid and Rudy and I meandered across the ice following Dad's trail. The brown splats of tobacco juice were frozen translucent on the river ice like drops from an errant paintbrush. The wind picked up a little; I put a hand on the top of Ma's hat to keep it from being lifted off my head. My ears were nearly numb with cold, and it occurred to me that I should have worn my wool toque instead.

Rudy was holding a valentine that he had made for his fourth-grade teacher, Mrs. Kelchner. At the beginning of the school year

Rudy hadn't said too much about Mrs. Kelchner one way or the other. "She's okay," was all he'd say when Ma or Dad would ask.

Things had changed since Ma left. Rudy talked about Mrs. Kelchner a lot. "Mrs. Kelchner says . . ." and "Mrs. Kelchner thinks . . ." were two of his favorite sentence starters. At open-house night in November, he'd blushed and stammered when he'd introduced Mrs. Kelchner to Dad.

"Pleased to meet you, Mrs. Kelchner," said Dad, extending his hand.

"Good evening, Mr. Bloom." Mrs. Kelchner had grasped Dad's hand with her own plump one. She didn't look anything like Ma. She was one of those women who become rectangular as they get older. The shelf of her enormous bosom was the top of the rectangle, and her broad hips shaped the lower part. Her best feature was her silver gray hair, which was swept on to the top of her head in an enormous bun.

"Rudy is a good boy," said Mrs. Kelchner. "I'm not pleased with his efforts in spelling this year, however."

"We'll work on that," said Dad.

"Yes, ma'am," said Rudy. "I'll work real hard."

Mrs. Kelchner reached out and clasped Rudy to her side. One hand rested on his head briefly while the other pressed him against her. "I know you will, my dear." Then she let him go and motioned across the room. "Show your family the work you've done."

Mrs. Kelchner was a hugger. Rudy was smitten.

We began walking faster across the ice as the wind picked up, chins down and eyes squinting against the cold. Suddenly Rudy let out a yelp and began running downriver across the ice.

"Rudy!" barked Sid.

I saw the red valentine skittering across the ice, the wind keeping it fluttering just out of Rudy's reach. A deep rumble came from the ice beyond our feet as Rudy got farther away from Dad's safely marked trail. He jumped over a ridge where two chunks of ice had banged together like tectonic plates to make a miniature mountain range of ice.

"Rudy!" I yelled. "Leave it."

He ignored me and kept chasing after the valentine. He slipped and fell on his backside. Sid took a few jogging steps toward Rudy then stopped. We both heard the low rumble of the ice groaning beneath us.

"Moron," muttered Sid. "It'll be a friggin' cold swim."

Late winter and early spring were the most dangerous times on the ice. The unpredictable weather and the rise and fall of the river tide caused weak spots and hairline breaks in the ice. That's why we always followed Dad's trail. He got up early in the morning and walked across to shore, using a jill-poke to tap at dark spots as he went, spitting tobacco juice all the way. Dad had some kind of built-in ice sense he'd developed over the years to safely navigate from the lighthouse to shore and back. "I've got a feel for it, Weezie," he'd say. "Don't you go trying it."

Now Rudy was tearing off across ice unmarked by tobacco juice or prodded with Dad's pole. Anyone who fell through would be swept downriver under the ice by the river current.

"Rudy!" yelled Sid. "Get back here!" Rudy ignored him.

A shiver of fear ran up my back and came out my mouth as a shriek. "Rudy! Back to the path!"

He ignored me, too, and stood up. A tangle of dead trees stood out from the ice near the far shore. They had fallen into the river during a hurricane the previous September. The winds on the Long Island shore had gotten up to over a hundred miles an hour. Up here, the river tide had been five feet above normal, and the winds had whipped around the lighthouse and toppled trees along the shore.

The valentine was caught at the base of a large tree limb sticking up out of the ice. Rudy ran the fifty yards to the tree limb and slid to a stop. I saw him bend over and then turn toward us, the valentine a red flag waving over his head.

Sid spit on the ice. "Whoever it is, I hope she's worth it," he muttered.

"It's Mrs. Kelchner," I said.

"Mrs. Kelchner." Sid looked at me and shook his head. "Mrs. Kelchner?"

I nodded. "Mrs. Kelchner."

"Mrs. Kelchner." He rolled his eyes. "Does he know she's married?"

Rudy was nearly within earshot now, trotting back across the ice toward us. I giggled, relief flooding through me as Rudy got nearer.

"I think so, but I guess he figures, you never know, right?"

A picture of Rudy and Mrs. Kelchner sitting at the kitchen table eating dinner flashed through my mind. She hugged him to her side, his head pressed alongside her bosom.

I glanced at Sid and our eyes met. Maybe he had the same mental picture as me. A giggle rose up and I tried to squelch it, but then Sid started laughing and I was gone. I saw Rudy introducing Mrs. Kelchner to Dad again: "Hi, Dad, this is my new wife, Mrs. Kelchner."

"Got it!" called Rudy.

Still laughing, I looked up just as a sharp *crack!* came from the ice under Rudy's feet. I saw him tilt backward a little and flail his arms, the red of the valentine in his hand flashing like a cardinal against the gray of the winter sky.

Across the distance between us, I could see the look of surprise and fear on Rudy's face as he realized what was happening. Buoyed by cakes of ice beneath his feet, he fell in slowly. First his boots, then his legs disappeared. When the river reached his thighs and the current took him, he fell forward and began to grab at the ice surface around the hole, desperately trying for a handhold against the slippery, gray surface.

"Hang on, Rudy!" yelled Sid as he took off running toward him.

I sprinted behind, laughter gone, heart hammering in my chest, and the raspy sound of my own breathing echoing through my head.

Chapter Twenty-two

IT WAS NO GOOD. I watched Rudy go under as we ran.

I screamed. I know I did because I can still hear the way my voice got swallowed up by the wind blowing past me over the hole in the ice where Rudy used to be.

Sid was holding on tight above my elbow as we both stood and stared at that dark hole in the ice.

There was nothing we could do except stare and hope that Rudy, in his panic, would remember the things that Dad had taught us about being under the ice. Both Sid and I had fallen in before. The trick was to look up and grab the rough underside of the ice and work your way, hand over hand, back to the hole. I remembered the dark and cold, the silence beneath the ice, then pushed the thought away.

"Get Dad," said Sid.

I ran, breathing Rudy's name with every step—"Rudy, Rudy, Rudy, Rudy"—as if my will alone could help him climb out from under the ice.

The lighthouse had never seemed so far away. The dots of tobacco slipped past, but the lighthouse didn't get any closer. I tore Ma's hat off, clutching it in my fist as I ran.

Finally I was at the bottom of the ladder. "Dad!" I screamed. "Dad!"

I scrambled up the ladder. "Dad!"

Dad burst out onto the deck, his coat already on. "What is it?"

"Rudy fell in," I gasped. Suddenly I could barely gather enough air to speak.

Dad pulled me up the last rung and onto the deck. He grabbed a hooked pole from against the wall and went down the ladder. I watched him run across the ice toward Sid's stick figure.

"Weezie?"

I spun around. Clayton was standing behind me. I took him by the shoulder and steered him inside.

"Rudy fell in," I said. "He'll need dry clothes. Up in his dresser."

"Is he okay, Weezie?"

"Dad'll get him out. Rudy knows what to do."

"What if he doesn't?" He grabbed a handful of my coat sleeve, and I'm ashamed to say I pushed his hand off before I went into the house.

"Dad and Sid'll get him out. But he's gonna be cold. Go get those clothes." Wide-eyed, Clayton turned and went upstairs.

I ran into the kitchen and added some coal to the fire. I threw off my coat and got blankets from the chest under the stairs.

"Hurry up with those clothes, Clayton!"

Suddenly the deck door banged open, and there was Rudy dangling wet and shivering between Sid and Dad.

They took him into the kitchen. Dad and Sid began to remove his dripping clothes.

"My fingers don't work," said Rudy. He grabbed at the buttons on the front of his sodden coat. His teeth clattered together so hard I could hear them from across the room.

"I don't expect they would," said Dad. He unbuttoned Rudy's coat and lifted it off his shoulders.

Sid gave Rudy a gentle shove as he pulled Rudy's shirt over his head. "You're frozen stiff, you moron."

I grabbed the soggy coat and shirt off the floor and carried them in to the laundry. Clayton passed in the hallway with an armload of dry clothes higher than his head. I stayed in the laundry and put the coat through the wringer. I wasn't Ma, and a boy, even a brother, needs privacy now and then.

As I walked back into the kitchen, Dad was pulling a big pair of wool socks over Rudy's feet. He was huddled on a chair pulled up close to the stove, wrapped in blankets but still shivering. His lips were blue.

Clayton stood to one side of Rudy staring at him and absent-mindedly wiping his nose with the back of his hand. His nose wasn't running—he doesn't have allergies in the winter—but he does that when he's nervous.

"He's okay, Clayton," I said. "You're okay, aren't you, Rudy?"

Rudy just stared at the stove.

"Here." I handed Clayton a towel. "Dry off his hair."

"I guess you woke us all up pretty good, son," said Dad. He tipped Rudy's boots upside down and put them on the drying rack hanging over the stove.

"Did you save the valentine?" asked Sid.

Rudy shook his head.

"Figures," said Sid. He lifted the soapstone off the stove, wrapped it in newspaper, and put it on the floor under Rudy's feet.

I grabbed the already steaming teakettle from its place on the stovetop and poured a cup of tea.

Rudy took it and held the hot mug between his hands. "That was stupid." His voice came out in a small squeak.

"We're just glad you're all right, boy," said Dad. "No stupid about it." He clapped Rudy on the back. His hand made a dull, hollow thump against the layers of blankets.

Rudy sipped the tea with a grimace and swallowed. "It's dark under there."

"There's easier ways to get out of school, Rudy," said Sid.

"Yeah, like throwing up," said Clayton. He rolled his eyes as if anyone could have thought of that.

"That would work," said Dad. He laughed gently.

"Or step on a nail!" said Clayton.

"You could of broke a leg," said Sid. "That would be effective."

"How about the trots?" said Dad. "I'd a let you stay home for that."

Rudy cracked a smile, then started laughing and shivering so hard he sloshed the tea. We were all laughing, and Clayton started hopping up and down. "I got the trots! I got the trots!"

Our laughter tickled its way up along the walls and into the top of the lighthouse, chasing away the emptiness there.

That night Rudy pulled his mattress off the top bunk and put it on the floor.

"Afraid you'll fall off?" asked Sid. We had gathered in the doorway to watch Rudy wrestle with the mattress as he tried to pull it down.

"Don't like the ceiling in my face, is all," said Rudy. He

grunted as he tried to pull the awkward weight of the mattress. It was caught on the metal edge of the bed.

"Don't strain anything," said Sid.

I hit Sid in the arm and scowled at him. I stepped into the room and grabbed onto the mattress. Rudy and I struggled with the mattress, switching positions and grips several times without success. Clayton pushed against the underside of the mattress as his contribution to the effort.

"What a pathetic bunch of chumps." Sid pushed us aside and grabbed the mattress. "Look out, Clayton." With one lunge, he lifted the mattress, slid it off the bed, and swung the lumpy mass down onto the floor.

"Yay, Sid!" said Clayton.

"Thanks, Sid," said Rudy.

"Yeah, Tom Mix to the rescue," said Sid. "That's me."

"And for this morning, thanks for . . . this morning." Rudy swallowed and looked at Sid.

"We're not losing anybody else," said Sid.

We looked at one another standing around the mattress on the floor. "Nobody else," I nodded.

"Hiyo Silver!" screeched Clayton. He dove forward and landed with an *oof* on the mattress.

Rudy yelped and dove on top of him. Sid and I glanced at each other, and suddenly we were all rolling around on the floor, giggling and wrestling and tickling like we were all five years old right along with Clayton.

"What's all this commotion?" Dad was standing in the doorway scowling at us.

For a second we all froze, worried about what he was going

to say. Dad grinned. "Do you need me to take ahold of you?"

Clayton screeched again and tried to escape out the door past Dad. Dad grabbed him and lifted him into the air. Clayton squealed, and it was the best sound in the world.

Now April fills the river to the brim
And drives the sea back upon the sea.
A hundred brooks and creeks and kills
Come rushing, tumbling down from hills,
The coves and marshes spring once more to life
And bays lie sparkling in the April sun.
—WILLIAM F. GEKLE, *A Hudson Riverbook*

Chapter Twenty-three

RUDY SLEPT ON THE FLOOR FROM THEN ON. He didn't like the feeling of being closed in. Guess being under the ice was something that never really left his mind.

Turns out that was the end of the ice, anyway. In the two weeks after Valentine's Day, the weather warmed, and although we had a cold snap that spring and even a couple of snowstorms in March, the ice was gone from the river.

I stood on the deck often that spring, leaning against the railing with the giddy April wind tugging at my hair. I watched the murky after-winter water, muddy with river-bottom silt and the runoff from a thousand upriver farms and towns. The spring river rushed past the lighthouse, heaving snowmelt and jetsam against the foundation. The water pushed its wet hands against the lighthouse foundation and flopped its muddy fists up against the shore.

When other things—birds, people, the sun—are in a hurry to leave, waving and rushing to be on their way, they are gone. The birds fly south, pushed by the wind; people leave for something better, happier, more exciting; the sun sets and moves to light another part of the earth, leaving darkness and gathering coolness. Only the river can run by, traveling to the distant sea past all the towns and bridges and trees on its way, and still remain here at the lighthouse. The river gets its cake and eats it, too: leaving and yet staying, arriving and simultaneously going, heaving and sighing in an endless, effortless rhythm.

Standing there by the railing, I saw the curve of the Hudson shore and the familiar buildings along the waterfront. I felt love for this small piece of the river and the land attached to it. I knew that if I could spend the rest of my days there leaning against the railing, listening to the rush and hum of the river, I would be content. If I could have my cake and eat it, too, I would have the sights of the world come to me while I stayed here and listened to the river speak. It would tell me all the stories I need to know.

That May we got a postcard from Ma. It had a picture of a many-storied house on the front with a sign above the porch that said ROOMS AND FAMILY-STYLE MEALS.

Dear Kids, [Ma wrote]
Am overseeing a boardinghouse in Willows, California. Very interesting and enjoyable. The weather is most agreeable to me, and the countryside is filled with beauty. Hope all is well in the lighthouse. I remain your loving mother.

"Isn't that just the cat's pajamas," said Sid sarcastically. "Maybe we can all go visit and have a Family-Style Meal."

The sadness inside me, which I thought had gotten smaller over the winter, blossomed again into an ugly, aching flower. I looked at the picture on the postcard and tried to imagine Ma there on the porch. She had a life without us, then.

"What's a boardinghouse?" asked Clayton. We were all sitting in Clayton and Rudy's room, Sid on the bottom bunk and the rest of us on Rudy's mattress.

I flipped the postcard back over to the picture side. "People rent rooms. It's a little like a hotel only people stay longer and they all eat together."

"Family style," said Sid.

Rudy reached over and took the postcard from me. "She's being mother for other people."

"She is not!" I stood up. Three faces looked up at me, startled. "She's got to make a living somehow, doesn't she?" Silence. "Well, doesn't she? What else does she know how to do besides cook and clean and keep house?"

"Geez, Louise, you don't have to yell."

"I'm not yelling!"

"Why are you defending her anyway?" said Sid. "She should be cooking and cleaning and keeping house here. Not in some boardinghouse."

"That's exactly what I'm talking about!"

"What?" Sid's voice was rising. "What exactly are you talking about?"

"You think Ma is your servant. Like the only thing she's good for is cleaning up and cooking for you!"

"I didn't see you complaining about Ma doing your laundry."

"Is that all you miss? The laundry being done?" I was yelling now.

"Stop fighting." It was Clayton. He sniffled and looked from Sid to me with those enormous green eyes of his.

"Stop sniveling, Clayton." My voice was hard. "You're always sniffling and crying. We're all tired of it."

"You should talk, Louise," said Rudy. "Going everywhere in that stupid old hat." He wrapped an arm around Clayton's shoulders.

I put a hand protectively against my hat. "Oh, I get it: everybody against Louise! Thanks a lot, Rudy."

"Well, you're being a moron," shouted Sid.

"You're the moron!" I screamed. "You're all morons!"

I ran across the hall to my bedroom and fell on my stomach across the bed. I was so angry and sad I thought my body might explode. Tears, hot and stinging, spilled out from the corners of my eyes.

I ripped the hat off and threw it from me. It landed with a soft thud on the braided rug. A second later, I scrambled off the bed and picked the hat up off the floor. I sat on the bed and stared at the hat in my hands. The fabric flowers were crumpled and folded. A piece of the straw piping had come loose on the back. I felt it between my thumb and finger. My tears fell onto the hat and disappeared into the weave of the straw. I kept staring at the hat as my vision blurred. The flowers dissolved into a cloud of pink, and I realized that no matter how much I wore it, the hat would always be Ma's, not mine.

Sitting there on the bed with my tears soaking into that old straw hat with faded flowers, I decided that I would find a way to make my heart whole, even if I never saw my mother again.

Chapter Twenty-four

ALONG WITH THE BOARDINGHOUSE POSTCARD, Ma
had sent something for Dad this time, too. When I had finally
stopped crying, I put the hat back on my head and stood up. I
wasn't ready to take it off for good, not quite yet. My eyes felt
puffy and gritty. Did tears have dirt in them? I wondered. Perhaps they carried away the sorrow and hurt inside you as little
pieces of hardness, like grains of sand in a glass of water.

Downstairs, Dad was sitting at the kitchen table reading a letter. He looked up at me when I walked in.

"Well, that's that," said Dad. His voice was a tired whisper.

"What is it, Dad?"

He didn't answer, but folded the letter and slid it back into
its envelope. "The boys still upstairs?"

I shrugged.

"Sounded like you were having words earlier."

I shrugged again.

"Your mother had her own reasons for leaving, Weezie. You
kids had nothing to do with it."

I looked at the floor. "Then why weren't we enough to make
her stay?" I said. My lip began to tremble, and I bit down on it.
I had cried enough over Ma.

Dad walked to me and touched my shoulder. "You four kids

are the strongest, prettiest, smartest, bravest goddamn bunch of children in the world."

I grabbed Dad around the waist and squeezed. The rough cloth of his shirt felt good against my swollen eyes, and the warmth of his body carried a solid comfort.

"You're enough to make me stay, come hell or high water. You hang on to that. I know it's not enough right now, but someday it might be." We stayed that way for a while. Dad's breathing, steady and slow, echoed through his chest. Dad cleared his throat and kissed me on the cheek. "Let's round up your brothers. I need to talk to you together."

We all gathered in the sitting room. It was like a regular meeting that Dad has with the lighthouse inspector or other visiting officials. One time the City Council selectmen came and had a meeting about right-of-way on the river and sat in our sitting room. Today it was just us Bloom kids sitting on the sofa and the rocking chair. Dad sat in the big wing chair by the window.

"Well," said Dad. "This is the thing. Your mother sent me a letter which I received today."

"We got a postcard," said Clayton. "About a boardinghouse."

Dad nodded. "Yes, boy, I know that." He cleared his throat. "Your ma is happy where she is out in California. She's doing real well, and she would like to stay out there. She wants to settle in California."

"We're going to move to California?" said Rudy. He was suddenly smiling. My heart gave a flutter. The three of us older kids all started talking at once. California? Clayton kind of bounced up and down on the edge of the rocking chair. California! They called it the Golden State. Before I could get a clear picture of what that might be like, Dad put his hand up. He shook his head.

"Hold on. We're not going to California." We all slumped back down against the sofa.

"Your ma didn't write to invite us to California. She wants me to divorce her," said Dad.

You might have thought there would be lots of shouting and crying and carrying-on after Dad said that, but there wasn't. We'd done our yelling upstairs earlier. Instead we were silent. You could almost hear the gears turning inside our heads. Rudy sighed. I looked at the floor. My eyes followed the words on the edge of the little round sitting-room rug. The words circled around a lovely pattern of leaves, flowers, and animals. The rug whispered to me, "Winter becomes spring becomes summer becomes fall becomes winter . . ." And around and around and around.

"That ain't much of a surprise," said Sid. He got up and walked out of the sitting room.

I looked at Dad sitting by the window. This was our family now.

"I'm sorry, Dad," I said.

He just nodded and gave me a little smile.

It was a short meeting.

Chapter Twenty-five

THE SHAD STARTED RUNNING IN EARLY APRIL. Sid was out on the rocks below the lighthouse every day. He'd go out early in the morning and fish until it was time to leave for school. He'd drop a line again as soon as we got home, sometimes off the rocks, sometimes out in the punt. When he's fishing is the only time I can say that I've seen Sid look really happy. He doesn't just fish to put food on the table, he really and truly enjoys it.

I've never understood the allure of fishing. It just seems like a lot of waiting for something to happen, as far as I can see. And I've had enough of that particular feeling lately.

Sid—and Rudy, too—see the whole operation as a challenge. It's them against the fish. The same Sid who forgets his homework and couldn't multiply fractions if his life depended on it can remember what bait, rod, and line he was using and the exact spot where he caught any given fish in the past three years. The same brain that can't remember the capitals of the fifty states can recite by memory dozens of lures and the fish they are designed to attract. Sid can debate the merits of live bait versus lure fishing ad nauseam and tell you what influence the tides have on all the species of fish that are in the river. The teacher who can figure out how to connect arithmetic or English composition with fishing will have Sid in the palm of her hand. So far that hasn't happened.

Of all the fishing that Sid does on the river, spring, summer, winter, and fall, his favorite is shad fishing. He's certainly told us that often enough.

Shad don't eat when they're swimming upriver to spawn, so you've got to trick them into striking a dart. Sid's got a knack for it. I've seen him stand right next to Baldy Hanscombe on the rocks, both of them using the same color dart, same rod, same everything, and Sid will pull in a dozen shad while Baldy's dart keeps coming up empty.

"What is it with you and shad?" Baldy will ask.

"Dunno," Sid will answer. "Just got a feel for it, I guess."

I've seen him stand patiently and try to teach Baldy or Rudy what it is exactly that he's doing to hook the fish. I'm not sure it's something you can explain in words, though. Either you've got a feel for where the dart's got to go ("Sometimes in the current, sometimes out, sometimes mid-depth in the water, sometimes not," says Sid to Rudy, who is reeling in, reeling out, trying to find the depth Sid is talking about) and a feel for that shad bumping the dart, that instant when you've got to jerk the line ("Not too much or too little, too fast or too slow," says Sid to Baldy, who is looking annoyed) and plant the hook—either you've got a feel for it, or it's something you aspire to. Sid's got a feel for it. Baldy and Rudy—and Dad, too—aspire. They catch shad, I'm not saying they don't. But not like Sid.

Sid takes most of his shad to shore and sells it. Roe shad sell for a dollar each; buck shad get a quarter. Rudy and Dad sell theirs, too. As Dad says, every little bit helps. Sid gives most of his shad money to Dad, but a fair amount of it goes to fishing tackle and dart makings in order to catch more shad.

And what the boys don't sell, we eat. We've always got as much shad as we can eat from the time they first start up the river with the blooming of the shadbush to the end of the lilac run. We have baked shad, broiled shad, smoked shad, and boiled shad. Roe with scrambled eggs for breakfast and salted roe steamed in bacon spread on toast. Somehow we never get tired of it.

The first shad run the spring after Ma left was something spectacular. It was late April and the shadbush was in bloom all along the river. People were on the banks of the river and in boats at all hours, from before dawn to after dark. The commercial fishermen had their nets out, but most folks were pulling the fish in one at a time on a line.

One afternoon after school, I was watching Sid from the deck as he fished off the rocks, and decided to try my hand at it. I took one of the darts that I had made—a pretty orangey color with a sprig of deer hair tied on the end—and took Dad's rod from its place by the back door, then climbed down onto the rocks.

"Hey, Sid."

He glanced over at me and then back at his rod. "Hey, Louise."

"How's the fishing?"

Sid poked his chin toward a basket nearby. "Middling. Three bucks and a roe."

"I was thinking I might like to try catching one." I held up the dart so he could see. "Thought I might try this pretty dart here."

Sid gave me a rare grin. "Step right up."

I tied the dart to the end of the line and cast out into the river. The dart entered the water with a jaunty *ploink* and sank out of sight. I turned the reel enough to stop the line and settled in for the wait.

"They're running a little deep today," said Sid.

I nodded and stared at the point where my dart had gone into the water. I couldn't tell how deep the dart was in the river. I decided to leave it to chance. If I had managed to float my pretty orange dart with the deer-hair tail in just the right place and a fish made a strike, then I'd be ready. If my dart remained unnoticed, only to float aimlessly in the river current somewhere out of the rush of migrating shad, I would be ready for that as well.

After several minutes, my mind began to wander. I realized once again that I just didn't have the right mind to be a fisherman. I am not patient enough or single-minded enough to focus on the possibility of fish below the surface of the river when so many things call to me from above its surface. The lazy swoop of a heron, the echoing calls of people along the shore, the churning passage of a tugboat up the river all served to distract me from the rod and line in my hands.

I turned my gaze upriver toward a boat with several rods sticking like insect antennae from its stern and felt a faint tremble in my own rod. I jerked the rod and felt a solid resistance on the end of the line. My heart sank. Had I been floating the dart so deep that I had snagged a log or some such on the bottom?

"Rats."

I yanked again, and the line moved sideways. A tremble of excitement skittered up my arms. "I got one!"

"Okay," said Sid, reeling in his own line. "Don't try to bring it in too fast. You don't want to lose it."

"What do I do?"

"You're doing fine, Weeze. Youse gotta play with it a little. Get her tired."

"It's a she?"

"I think so. See how it's swimming? Into the channel like that? It's a roe."

My arms had started to ache already.

"Weezie's got a fish!" I heard Clayton's voice from the deck.

I had reeled in several feet of line by the time Rudy and Clayton came scrambling down over the rocks to watch. My heart was thumping hard against my chest, and I could feel a tremble in my fingers as I worked the reel.

"Look at her play that fish! You're a natural!" Sid laughed.

I understood now what Sid was waiting so patiently for as he cast his line again and again into the water. It was this feeling: excitement and a thrill of anticipation as we waited for the fish to be revealed from the brown depths of the river, and the shiver of anxiety that it might somehow slip off the hook before I could get it up to the surface.

A flash of silver passed, and Clayton squealed. "I see it!"

"That's it, Weezie!" Sid leaned down and scooped the silver fish into his net. The shad was magnificent—her silver scales flashed iridescent in the sunlight as she was lifted from the water. Her stomach bulged with its burden of roe. We stared at the fish.

"Biggest one I've seen this year," said Sid. He grinned at me.

"You take her, Sid. Sell her in town." I was panting a little from the excitement.

"No sirree, Bobby!" said Sid. "We're eating this one tonight."

We tromped up to the lighthouse, me holding the gently struggling shad by the gills.

Clayton skipped ahead of us up over the rocks to the deck. "Weezie got a shad! Dad! Weezie got a shad!"

Rudy clapped me on the shoulder. "Good going."

"Guess you'll have to make a few more of those orange darts," said Sid. "I'd take a couple two or three." He was still grinning. I couldn't help but grin back.

Dad met us in the kitchen.

"She's nine pounds, easy," said Dad. "Well, well, look at that. Sid's been telling you his secrets, Weezie." He smiled at me then winked at Sid. "Wish I could get him to tell me."

"Wasn't anything I told her," said Sid. "She did it on her own."

"Guess I just have a feel for it!" I turned and swung the fish into the sink. "Maybe I'll tell you and Rudy *my* secrets one of these days."

Everybody laughed, and I stood there looking at the beautiful fish, its silver sides shining like precious metal, and I realized we were all happy, thanks to this marvelous fish—the Blooms were happy and whole, even without Ma.

I said a silent thank-you to my lovely shad and all of its unseen brothers and sisters still swimming relentlessly up the river as the spring flowers blossomed along the shore.

Chapter Twenty-six

THE LAST SATURDAY IN MAY was the kind of day they write songs about. You could almost hear Louis Armstrong's ragged voice on the breeze.

"Blue skies, smiling at me
Nothing but blue skies do I see."

I was out on the deck with Clayton getting ready to paint the privy door. Dad poked his head out of the kitchen door and called to us.

"Put the paint away! No chores this morning."

"Yay!" Clayton didn't need any convincing. He dropped his brush and ran around the corner.

"Come on in the kitchen, Weezie. We're going on an outing."

I put the paint can and brushes inside the privy and went in the house. "Where are we going?"

Sid already had his fishing gear gathered under one arm, ready to go out the back door.

"Wait a minute, son," said Dad. "You're not fishing right now."

"You said no chores this morning," moaned Sid.

"Well, you'll need your fishing gear, but not here." Dad grinned. "We're going on a picnic."

"Someplace we'll have room to throw the football?" asked Rudy.

"Absolutely," said Dad. "We'll make sure of it."

"Hard-boiled eggs!" shouted Clayton. "I want hard-boiled eggs."

"Darn tootin'," said Dad. "All the hard-boiled eggs you can eat."

"Oh, c'mon, Dad, a picnic?" said Sid.

"Yes. A picnic. Time to get out of this lighthouse for a while," said Dad. "And you are going to enjoy it, Sidney." He clapped Sid on the back.

"C'mon yourself, Sid," I said. "You'll have your fishing rod. The sun's out, it's May, and we'll have hard-boiled eggs! What more do you want?"

Sid gave a laugh. "Guess you're right. I'll pack up some stuff."

"Rudy, get the punt ready," said Dad. "We're heading out in half an hour!"

Rudy went out to get the punt organized. Dad had fixed up an outboard motor that someone in town had given him, and it was attached to the punt. It was a little three-horsepower Johnson that made a high-pitched whirring sound as it churned the water behind the stern. Rudy had become the unofficial hand in charge of maintenance and upkeep on the Johnson. He spent hours tinkering with the little motor and taking the punt up and down the river on "test runs" to see if it might need a little more adjustment to the governor or the throttle so as to get it running just right.

I put on a pot of water to boil the eggs and gathered up some other things to eat: cheese, some crackers, and a jar of pickles. I filled a big canvas bag with the food and tucked the book I was currently reading along the side. Clayton came downstairs with his balsa-wood airplane and a toy tractor. They went into the bag.

"Rudy wanted his football, do you know where that is?" I asked.

"Yup." Clayton ran back up the stairs to get the football.

After the eggs were done and we had gathered all we wanted, we trundled into the punt and headed off upriver, Rudy at the tiller. The punt sat low in the water with all of us and the extra baggage, but the tide was leisurely and we moved slowly through the water without breaking waves.

We putted up the shoreline for twenty minutes or so, Sid trolling a line behind the boat just in case a fish might be tempted.

"There's a good spot!" I said. There was a nice stretch of sandy beach along the near shore.

"Looks like it," said Dad. Rudy steered the punt toward shore.

We scrambled out once the punt touched shore and set up our picnic. Sid commenced fishing as soon as he could, and Clayton got out his tractor and started plowing the beach.

Rudy and Dad threw the football. I took my book and sat with my back against a fallen tree and read. Clayton's motor noises and the hum of Sid's reel as he cast out, reeled in, cast out, reeled in, mingled with the sounds of the football as Rudy and Dad passed it back and forth. I could feel the warm sunshine and tried to soak it up and remember it so I could store it for later. Spring is a fickle season. But today was perfect picnic weather: warm and sunny with just a little whisper of a breeze tickling along the edges of the air.

I closed my book and shut my eyes and tried to feel the sun on each part of my body. I must have fallen asleep because the next thing I knew, Sid was telling me to come and get it. I opened my eyes and ran my tongue around my mouth to get the sleep out and walked over to the blanket they had spread on the sand.

I passed out the eggs and Dad sliced chunks of cheese for everyone. Sid poured the iced tea.

After lunch, Clayton and Rudy tried their luck at flying the balsa-wood plane. Then the three of us built a town of sticks and driftwood. Clayton made the roads with his tractor while Rudy and I stacked pieces of wood like cards to make the buildings. An empty soup can became a silo and an old shoe sole was the roof of the town hall.

Sid was still fishing, releasing everything he caught. He pulled in a couple of catfish. No shad, though. Dad was sitting on the pebbly edge of the beach near the water just watching the easy plop and tug of Sid's line in the water. There was a balsa-wood bobber on the line, and it danced and bobbed in the slow river current.

After a while, we all ended up sitting by Dad as Sid fished. The late afternoon sun winked against the water. A cormorant swam out near the middle of the river, its sleek black head crooked like a snake's against the low profile of its back.

"Sing a song, Weezie!" said Clayton.

"How about we all sing a song," I said. "We can do a round."

"What's a round?" asked Clayton.

"Youra head isa round," said Sid.

"Ahead what?" Clayton scowled at Sid.

Rudy rolled his eyes and Sid scrubbed the top of Clayton's head. "Never mind, you dope. It was a joke."

"We all sing the same song, but start it at different times. The tune kind of goes around and around," I said.

"I'm not singing," said Sid. He shook his head as he stared at the end of his fishing rod.

"Come on, Sid, please?" said Clayton. "Please, pleeeeeease?"

"Don't be a stick in the mud," said Dad. "We're all singing."

"Oh, for pity's sake," said Sid. But he reeled in his line.

"Here—we'll sit in a circle." I herded everyone back to the blanket. "And we're doing 'Row, Row, Row Your Boat.'"

"I know that song!" said Clayton. He started singing it.

"When I say 'row, row, row your BOAT,' you start. Then Rudy, then Sid, then Dad. And just keep singing."

I started the song.

"Row, row, row your boat gently down the stream . . ."

Clayton chimed in at the right spot, then Rudy, Sid, and Dad picked it up as it moved around to them. By the end of the first round, Clayton had lost his spot and was singing with me, but that was okay because there were still four parts.

"Merrily, merrily, merrily, merrily,
Life is but a dream."

The simple song twisted and floated around us, running in layers out toward the river and back in to shore. After several times around, I stopped and that was the signal for everyone else to stop as well. The end of a round is my favorite, when the silence becomes part of the singing. I listened to the complimentary layers of sound peel away one by one as Rudy finished, and then Sid. Finally it was only Dad's voice on the last "life is but a dream." The song faded away and left us smiling at one another.

There was applause behind us. We all turned to look up toward the road. "Bravo!" a man called, and waved. I stood and curtsied toward the road. Rudy bowed low next to me.

"Bravo!" echoed Clayton, raising his hands above his head in tight little fists.

Dad waved back, and the man continued on his way.

"Geez, a standing ovation," said Sid. "We oughta sell tickets next time."

There was that laughter again, sneaking up on us and spilling out into the air.

That picnic afternoon the May sunshine whispered of the hotter days of summer and warmed our faces as we sat on the little sandy beach; and the hope that we might someday come to be happy, in spite of our absent mother, warmed our spirits and gave lift to our slowly mending hearts.

There on the beach beside the lordly Hudson, for the first time I allowed myself to think that these happy moments might multiply and run together into a chain of happy days and nights, stretching out across that magic spring and into summer.

Cool shades and dews are around my way,
And silence of the early day;
Mid the dark rocks that watch his bed,
Glitters the mighty Hudson spread,
Unrippled, save by drops that fall
From shrubs that fringe his mountain wall;
And o'er the clear still water swells
The music of the Sabbath bells.
—WILLIAM CULLEN BRYANT,
"A Scene on the Banks of the Hudson"

Chapter Twenty-seven

SCHOOL LET OUT IN JUNE. None of us had missed a day of school since the end of March, which was something of a record for the kids from the lighthouse. Rudy was sad about leaving Mrs. Kelchner, but she assured him he could visit her classroom anytime next year even though he'd be in fifth grade.

Summer was the busiest time of year for river traffic. The day liner made several trips up and down the river each day. Barges and other big transport vessels passed by the lighthouse on their way to or from the Erie Canal at the top of the river in Troy. I imagined the Erie, stretching across the top of New York all the way to Buffalo, a channel of water connecting the great Lake Erie with the great Hudson River. We were a point along that enormous, gray-green highway. I was proud of my father and his job in keeping our part of the river safe.

In the middle of June, usually the first weekend after school got out, there was a boat race on the river. The race started under the Patroon Island Bridge in Albany and the finish line was in New York City. The little speedboats were sleek and fast, and people lined up all along the river to watch them speed by. The lighthouse deck was a perfect spot to watch from.

We'd invited a bunch of people from town to watch from the deck, and lots of other folks rowed out uninvited and sat on the rocks around the base of the lighthouse. Those we knew usually ended up on the deck. It was just after seven o'clock on a Sunday morning, and people had already started to row out to the lighthouse. The starting gun went off in Albany at 6 A.M., and the first racers would begin to reach our lighthouse by seven-thirty or so.

On this race day, the one with Ma gone, Sid was up on the light deck with Margaret Tomlinson. She had come out early with a wicker picnic basket full of food. Her father owned the hardware store in town. Mr. Tomlinson had dropped Margaret off at the lighthouse in their Chris-Craft boat, a beautiful, polished wooden thing that seemed to glide through the water without effort.

Everyone called Margaret "Tommy" except her parents and Sid. I waved up to them from my spot against the lower deck rail. "Hi, Tommy!"

She leaned over and waved back down at me, her bobbed hair blowing against her cheek. "Hi, Weezie!"

Sid didn't even glance down at me. He said something to Tommy and pointed toward the river. She followed with her eyes the direction his finger pointed and then nodded. I imagine Sid was telling her about one of the many times Dad had rescued a capsized racer and ferried them and the foundering craft to the lighthouse. And I was pretty sure that Sid's part in the rescues had taken on a greater significance than it might have given a different audience.

Clayton stood beside them on the rail. He was looking upriver, intent on being the first to shout out the approach of a racer.

Dad had rescued people more than once on race days past, and he was ready to do the same today if need be.

Rudy came up beside me. "You see them yet?"

I shook my head. "Clayton'll yell."

"Dad said I could help with a rescue today—if anyone goes in." Rudy drummed on the railing.

"You mean 'when.'"

Rudy rubbed his hands together. "You're darn tootin'! Somebody always swamps. I'm going down to the punt. See you!"

"See you."

I walked into the kitchen. Mr. Shufelt and Dad were sitting at the table. An open can of condensed milk sat on the table between them. The smell of coffee came from the aluminum percolator on the stovetop.

"Any boats yet?" asked Mr. Shufelt.

I shook my head. "Nothing yet."

"Well, it's only a little after seven. Still early."

I took a mug from the cupboard and filled it halfway with coffee then sat down at the kitchen table. I picked up the can and poured in milk until the mug was full.

"Having a little coffee with your milk?" said Dad.

"This is café au lait, Dad," I said. "It's very good. You should try it sometime."

"Perhaps I will," said Dad. "Probably not this morning, though."

I shrugged and took a sip of the coffee.

Rudy poked his head in the kitchen door. "I can't get the motor going, Dad."

"Why you need to be running her now, son?"

"I'm just getting ready. You know, in case someone needs help." Rudy looked from Dad to Mr. Shufelt. "Hiya, Mr. Shufelt."

"Rudy."

Rudy looked back at Dad. "Won't be good if someone's swamped and the motor won't start, Dad."

"D'you prime her?"

Rudy nodded.

"Adjust the governor?"

Another nod.

Dad put his coffee on the table and pushed his chair back. "All right, let's see what's going on with that motor."

Dad left and Mr. Shufelt and I were sitting alone at the table. I blew on my café au lait and took another sip.

"Not a bad day for a race," said Mr. Shufelt. I nodded.

"I expect someday Rudy will be out there racing himself."

I nodded again. "He does like that outboard." I felt my feet swinging under the table like a kid's and made them stop. My left toe banged against the chair leg and I winced. I took another sip of coffee and cleared my throat. I ran my hand along the zigzag outline of straw piping on the back of my hat, my fingers stopping at the place where it was loose.

"You knew Ma growing up, right?"

"Yes, I did," said Mr. Shufelt. "Myra Lane. Known her since first grade."

"What was she like?"

Mr. Shufelt raised his eyebrows. "I expect you know your ma better than I would, Louise."

"No, I mean as a kid. What was she like as a kid?"

"As a child?" Mr. Shufelt gave a little shrug. "Like any other, I suppose. She was a good girl, polite. Maybe a little stubborn. But that's to be expected in a New Century Baby. All us children born in 1900 were told we were something extra special from the day we arrived. Perhaps Myra took that a bit more to heart than some." He took a mouthful of coffee and stared off over my shoulder.

"What do you mean?"

"I dunno," said Mr. Shufelt. "She had a lonesome part to her, Myra. Like she was reserving part of her for something else, some other time. Something as special as she was, and it sure wasn't Hudson, New York."

I felt a heaviness on my shoulders, and I imagined Mr. Shufelt's words pressing there like enormous hands. Each syllable piling a little higher, pressing a little harder, making me want to lay my head on the table and sleep.

"Your ma left as soon as she graduated from high school. We were all surprised when she came back." He paused and looked into his coffee cup like he was seeing the past in there. "Guess she was pretty surprised, too. Probably thought marrying a lighthouse man would mean seeing the country. Atlantic Ocean, Great Lakes, California coast. Not coming back here . . ." His voice trailed off. "Right back here in the middle of the Hudson River." He muttered to his coffee. I wasn't sure he was still even talking to me. "Funny thing is, I think your dad requested it as a surprise for her."

I swallowed another mouthful of my café au lait. It tasted like cold, milky coffee. Nothing special.

"Guess I should go see if your father needs any help with that motor." Mr. Shufelt scraped his chair back from the table and stood up. I nodded.

"Your father is a good man, Louise. Don't you forget that." He walked to the kitchen door but turned back toward me before he went out. "And your ma, too. I know she loves you kids."

I nodded again and turned back to my coffee. I knew Ma loved us—but that wasn't enough to make her stay.

"Boat!" I heard Clayton yell from the light tower. "Boat coming!"

Chapter Twenty-eight

"BOAT, BOAT!" YELLED CLAYTON AGAIN.

I looked upriver and saw a slim boat bouncing toward us. The tide was coming in, so the boat was heading against the current as the driver came barreling down to the lighthouse. People along the shore waved and cheered. Many of them clanged cowbells that they had brought for the occasion. Several pleasure craft had docked at Hudson to watch the race, and one of them chugged out toward the middle of the river to get a closer look at the passing racers.

"Moron!" I heard Sid yell. "He'll kill somebody."

"Here comes another one!" Clayton yelled. A second racer, and then a third, emerged upriver, all bouncing along the water toward us at full speed.

I waved wildly from the railing as the first boat passed us. I squinted to read the name written on the bow. "Krazy Kat!" I shouted in greeting. "Go!" I watched Krazy Kat zip past, and listened to the high whining buzz, then deep thud, as the boat alternately rose into the air then landed on the water with each wave.

The little racing boats were small and shallow, and they rode on top of the water as if they were made of balsa wood. They skimmed the surface toward us like stones skipped along the water by some enormous hand.

"*Julie's Pride!*" I shouted. "*Water Bug! Intrepid!*" A gust of wind threatened to lift my hat off, and I put a hand on top to secure it. The names of the boats were as varied as their colors. Some were painted plain brown or black with a stripe, others marked with bright splashes of color that stood out against the gray river water: red, orange, yellow, and purple.

I looked below the railing and saw Rudy in the punt, making his way slowly around the lighthouse, waiting for the chance to use his new navigational skill with the outboard motor.

"Hey, Rudy," I called.

He grinned up at me and saluted.

The boats continued to whiz past, sporadically now in small clusters or one and two at a time. Some passed on the Athens side of the lighthouse; I could hear people cheering from the opposite shore.

Another pleasure boat, this one a small sailboat, moved out toward the middle of the river.

"Get out of there!" I heard Rudy yell from down below.

"They can't hear you, Rudy," I called. "Save your breath!"

"They shouldn't be there!" he called back. I could see the scowl lines between his eyebrows as he turned his head to yell to me.

"No use chasing after fools," I said softly as I watched the sailboat bob toward the racers. I thought of Ma, saw her standing at the railing watching last year's race, the wind from the river blowing wispy pieces of black hair around her face. Or Ma walking around and around the deck, a pot of coffee in one hand and a cluster of coffee mugs in the other. She had loved to laugh and visit with all the people lined up along the railing as she poured mug after mug of hot black coffee. The echo of her laugh still floated around the outside of the lighthouse, somehow staying on the wind that moved along the rough brick walls.

Where was Ma now? Leaning against a different railing in front of a boardinghouse somewhere in California. A sadness came over me as I looked out at the sailboat, the racers still skimming past every minute or two. The boats that had looked so fearless and adventurous just a few moments before now looked small and reckless.

"No use chasing after fools," I repeated. I decided I wasn't going to wonder about Ma anymore. If she was coming back, she was coming back. If she wasn't, she wasn't. No use worrying about it anymore. At the same time I knew a part of me would always wonder and be waiting.

"*Minnie Mouse!*" I yelled, and waved to a black-and-red racer skipping past the sailboat's bow.

My father and a tall man in a straw boater's hat were leaning on the railing downriver. It was Tommy's father, Mr. Tomlinson. I moved toward them, walking sideways so that I could still face the water as I moved. I stopped and propped myself on my forearms next to Dad. Our elbows touched, and I leaned over and put my head on his shoulder. The roughness of Ma's hat pressed against my ear, and I took it off.

Mr. Tomlinson craned his neck beyond Dad to look at me. "Hello there, Louise."

I lifted my head and smiled. "Good morning, Mr. Tomlinson."

"Perfect morning for a race," he said.

I nodded. "My favorite so far is *Krazy Kat.*"

"*Krazy Kat,*" Mr. Tomlinson repeated and grinned. "Fine choice. What about you, Owen? Any particular favorites this year?"

"I like them all," said Dad. He squinted out across the water. "Myra likes any of them that have yellow." He turned to me. "She always liked yellow, didn't she, Weezie?"

I nodded. I didn't feel like watching the boats anymore. "Would you like some coffee?"

"Sure, I'd have half a cup," said Dad.

"Mr. Tomlinson?"

"That's very kind of you, Louise, thank you."

I turned and went back into the lighthouse.

I poured Mr. Tomlinson's coffee in the turquoise blue mug with the handle made of two rings, one on top of the other. I was watching the coffee rise up toward the smooth turquoise rim of that mug, so I didn't see the collision. I heard it. There was a sickening thud and the sound of wood breaking. People on the lighthouse started to yell. And I heard Sid's voice over it all, calling Rudy's name.

Later, many weeks later, I threw the mug away so I wouldn't have to hear the thud and hear Sid yelling Rudy's name every time I looked at it.

Chapter Twenty-nine

OUTSIDE, DAD AND MR. TOMLINSON WERE GONE. I looked out across the water and saw that two boats had collided in the channel. People on the rocks below were scurrying around to gather on the Hudson side. Sid and Tommy burst through the kitchen door behind me.

"Rudy's hit!" said Sid. He grabbed the railing next to me and stared out across the channel. My stomach lurched and I clamped my lips together to fight the nausea. My eyes scanned the water for a sign of Rudy.

"I'm not standing here to watch," said Sid. He turned and walked toward the other side of the deck where the ladder was. I forced myself to turn away from the water and follow him.

"Wait! Sid!"

Clayton stepped out of the kitchen and grabbed at my hand. I clasped it absently and pulled him along as I followed Sid. "Sid, where's Dad?"

"He's going out there," said Sid.

On the other side of the deck, Mr. Tomlinson's shiny mahogany Chris-Craft was already moving from the dock. Dad was standing next to Mr. Tomlinson. The boat cleared the corner of the lighthouse, then surged forward toward the channel. Mr. Shufelt met us at the top of the ladder.

"Your dad'll be to Rudy in short time."

Sid made to push Mr. Shufelt aside and get to the ladder. "I'm taking your skiff. They might need two."

Mr. Shufelt put out a hand. "Won't be a help to get any more boats out there, Sidney."

"I'm going!"

"No, son. Your dad needs to focus on one thing right now, and that's Rudy. You do him a favor and stay put right here."

"I want to help!"

"Your dad has pulled more people from this river than anyone," said Mr. Shufelt. "He knows what he's doing. Now, if you really want to be a help, get some blankets and coffee ready so whoever gets pulled from the river can get warmed up!"

Sid made a sound in his throat as if he meant to argue some more, but he turned and walked into the lighthouse.

I hurried back to the other side of the deck, still holding on to Clayton. Tommy was still there against the railing. She turned toward me as we approached, and I could see that she was crying.

"He went out to tell that sailboat to get out of the way," she said. "Stupid people."

I looked out across the channel. Dad and Mr. Tomlinson had reached the spot where the boats had collided. I watched Dad bend over the side of the boat and pull someone from the water. Was it Rudy? My heart was pounding in my temple and I realized that I still had hold of Clayton's hand. He was silent.

"A racer hit him just before he got to the sailboat," said Tommy. "Bright yellow."

We watched helplessly from the railing as Mr. Tomlinson's boat moved around in a circle out in the channel. A second person in the water was swimming toward the boat. I strained to see if it was Rudy who grabbed Mr. Tomlinson's hand and was pulled up into the boat. The first person they had pulled from the river was hidden somewhere on the floor of the boat. I could see Dad's back hunched over as he bent down to talk to the person.

"He'll be coming back now," I said. "We'll see how Rudy got banged up this time. It's always Rudy getting in some kind of calamity." I tried to keep my voice light, but I could hear my words ringing false in my own ears.

Instead of heading back to the lighthouse, Mr. Tomlinson steered the boat toward the Hudson shoreline. The boat surged ahead, spitting out a vee of white water at her stern.

"Where are they going?" asked Clayton. It was the first thing he'd said since emerging from the lighthouse.

"Municipal dock," said Tommy.

As she spoke, I heard the high, insistent wail of a siren and the town ambulance pulled onto the dock. Racers continued to pass on both sides of the lighthouse, and the people on the Athens shore yelled. The shouts and ringing cowbells sounded distant and faint. It seemed as if there was a thickness of air around me muffling the sounds coming toward me from the shore.

The boats sped by, oblivious to the collision that had taken place just a few minutes before. A tugboat had moved upriver to steer racers around and clear the debris out of the water.

The three of us stood silently at the railing, straining to see what was happening on the riverbank.

"Is he okay, Weezie?" asked Clayton.

I shook my head vaguely, keeping my eyes on the Hudson dock. "I don't know." Clayton began to cry quietly and I squeezed his hand. "The ambulance men will take a look at him and make sure he's all right." I spoke with more conviction than I felt. Whoever had swum to the boat was probably okay. But the one Dad had pulled from the river and put on the bottom of the boat was probably hurt much worse. Which one was Rudy?

Mr. Tomlinson's boat pulled up to the dock, and I saw figures scrambling to secure it. The ambulance men approached the boat, and a person was lifted up from the boat and taken to the ambulance. A second person, wrapped in a blanket, climbed out of the boat and sat down on the dock. *Please let that be Rudy. Let the sitting person be Rudy.* I silently prayed.

Then Dad climbed out of the boat and ran to the ambulance. He climbed in, and the big doors on the back of the ambulance closed. That was when I knew that Rudy would need more than blankets and coffee to warm him.

Chapter Thirty

SID CAME BACK OUT OF THE LIGHTHOUSE with an arm-load of blankets.

"We don't need the blankets, Sid," I said.

Mr. Tomlinson's boat was nearly back to the lighthouse. Sid dropped the blankets on the deck and scrambled down the ladder to catch the bowline.

"Is Rudy okay?" I called down.

Mr. Tomlinson didn't answer, but motioned us down. "Get in the boat, kids, I'll get you to the hospital. Margaret—you, too."

I started toward the ladder, then remembered the lighthouse. "We've got to lock up."

Mr. Tomlinson shook his head. "You'd best come now, Louise." His tone made my heart ache. Rudy was in bad trouble.

Somehow Mr. Shufelt was standing next to me. I felt his hand on my shoulder. "You go ahead, Louise, and don't worry about the light. I'll lock up here."

I swallowed the lump in my throat and climbed after Clayton down the ladder. I jumped across the space from the ladder to the boat and felt Ma's hat fly off. I yelped and tried to grab at it as I landed in the bottom of the boat but could only watch as it sailed out into the river.

"My hat!" For one frantic second, I considered jumping in after it. The next second I was holding the gunwale and all I was thinking about was Rudy.

"Sit down, everyone!" said Mr. Tomlinson.

Mr. Tomlinson steered his boat away from the lighthouse and toward the Hudson Marina and Yacht Club. He docked the boat there and we all climbed into his shiny black Packard.

On another day, I might have been thrilled to be riding in a car so elegant and modern. The dashboard was like I imagined the cockpit of a plane would look: dials and gauges blinked and whirred importantly as Mr. Tomlinson pushed the starter button next to the steering wheel.

None of us spoke on the ride to the hospital. Clayton started crying again as the car bounced along Route 32. "I'm scared," he said. "He's going too fast."

I looked out at the trees and houses whipping past at forty-five miles an hour. "Close your eyes," I whispered.

The hospital was a long, two-story brick building atop a hill on the edge of town. A hundred windows stared down at us as we walked quickly across the parking lot to the front entrance.

The nurse at the front office wouldn't let us in to see Rudy. She wouldn't even tell us where he was.

"Please have a seat," she said. Her white hat had two corners pointing out like smoothed-down horns on the back of her head.

"These children are here to see their brother," said Mr. Tomlinson. "He was injured on the river. I'm sure the ambulance got here not long before us."

"Please have a seat," the nurse repeated. She made her mouth into something like a smile. "I'll find out what I can."

The waiting area had several high-backed wooden chairs placed around the walls. End tables were set between the chairs here and there. A radio played softly in the corner. Clayton and I sat on the far wall still holding hands. Sid sat opposite us nearest the nurses' station. Tommy sat next to Sid, and Mr. Tomlinson settled on the next wall.

I blindly took a magazine from the end table next to me. It was a *Ladies' Home Journal*. A blond woman in a white dress with red polka dots was on the cover. Her hands were clasped together against her forehead. She had pretty pink fingernails. A man leaned in close to her. Only half his head was in the picture.

I released Clayton's hand. He wiped his nose with the back of his other hand and slumped against me. I put the magazine back on the table and put my arm around Clayton's shoulders. I could feel his back rising and falling with his breathing. The radio was broadcasting the *RCA News Hour*. It was only eight o'clock in the morning.

"When are they going to tell us something?" said Sid. "It ain't right to make us sit here."

Mr. Tomlinson shifted forward in his chair. "They'll tell us as soon as they know something, son. The important thing is them attending to Rudy, not to us. Hard as it is, we're just going to have to wait."

Sid grunted and scowled but remained in his seat. Tommy placed her hand on his arm and whispered something to him. Sid nodded and stared down into his lap. He put his hand over her hand on his arm, and they just sat there like that. I looked away out the window. There were bars on the window, and I had time to wonder why before the phone at the nurses' desk rang. I watched the nurse pick up the phone and look over at us as she listened to whatever the person on the other end was saying. My heart started beating fast, and I took Clayton's hand again.

The nurse hung up the phone and walked over to the waiting area. Her white-stockinged legs made a swishing sound as she walked. She didn't talk to any of us children, but to Mr. Tomlinson. "You were inquiring about a patient named Bloom?"

"Yes," said Mr. Tomlinson. "Rudolph Bloom."

"He's in the east wing. I'll direct you."

"How is he?" asked Sid. "Can you tell us that?"

The nurse shook her head. "I'm sorry I can't give you any information. He's in the critical-care wing, however. It was a boating accident?"

"Yes," said Mr. Tomlinson.

The nurse nodded primly. "Kids in boats. I could tell you stories. Young people today are reckless."

Mr. Tomlinson raised a hand. "This young man was not. Where can we find him, please?"

The nurse raised her eyebrows and pursed her lips as if to say something, but apparently thought better of it. "The east wing is to your left." She pointed toward a long corridor. "Take this hallway to the end, first right-hand turn through double doors."

Dad was sitting in a waiting area in the next wing that was almost identical to the one we had just left. High-backed chairs lined three walls. Everything was white and light green.

The morning ticked away as we waited. I tried to imagine racing boats still humming by the lighthouse but couldn't. Surely the world wasn't going on about its business as usual while we sat silent and frightened in the white-and-green limbo of the hospital waiting room.

Mr. Tomlinson left around noon and returned with sandwiches wrapped in waxed paper and a jug of iced tea. None of us ate much.

A little while later, a man in a white coat emerged from the corridor and approached us.

"Mr. Bloom?"

"Yes," said Dad. He stood up and walked to meet the doctor. "How is he? How is Rudy?"

The doctor looked at Dad and then at the three of us huddled around him. He didn't smile, but he looked kind. "Sit down, please, Mr. Bloom. I'm Dr. Solomon." He took Dad by the arm and guided him back toward the chair.

Dad shook his head. "I'll stand. Tell me."

Dr. Solomon cleared his throat. There was a dark red spot on the cuff of his white coat. My eyes followed it as his hands moved. I couldn't look away from it.

"Your son was very badly injured," Dr. Solomon said softly. He looked right at Dad as he spoke. "Severe head trauma and internal injuries. He also aspirated a great deal of water, which added to the trauma to his system." He paused. "We tried everything we could. I'm sorry. There was nothing I could do to save him."

Suddenly there was a rushing sound in my ears, and my head felt light. I thought I might faint. I sat down in a chair and closed my eyes. Rudy was dead. Hit by a yellow boat and tossed into the gray Hudson River. I didn't feel anything but a vague unease. A sense that this wasn't really happening. Maybe I was dreaming this doctor, this hospital, this world of white and green where my brother's dead body, bruised and broken, lay somewhere nearby in a room down the hall.

Dimly I heard Clayton crying. I felt him climb into my lap. I opened my eyes. *Rudy*, I called out silently. *Don't leave. You can't leave.*

Sid kicked the chair next to me, and it tipped over sideways, knocking into one of the end tables. Iced tea splattered onto the floor. Dad righted the chair and gently pushed Sid to sit in it. He pulled another chair up in front of us and sat down facing the three of us, Sid and me side by side, Clayton in my lap. Then Dad leaned forward and put his arms around us. We were a circle of Blooms with too many pieces missing.

I felt Dad's shoulders quake, and suddenly the tears were pouring out of me. A sadness like nothing I had ever known shook my body and escaped out my eyes in salty, stinging tears. It came out from my lungs in deep, choking sobs against my father's neck.

We sat there huddled in the waiting room, our waiting over and the grieving just begun.

Chapter Thirty-one

RUDY'S FUNERAL WAS TO BE HELD WEDNESDAY at the Dutch Reformed Church.

We were gathered in the lighthouse sitting room. Rudy had been dead almost twenty-four hours.

"Ma ought to be here," said Sid. "It ain't right."

"What was the name of that boardinghouse?" Dad asked. His voice was soft and raspy, like he could barely draw a deep enough breath to make his vocal cords vibrate.

"Don't know," I said. "But it's in Willows, California."

"I've got to go into town to make arrangements." Dad pushed himself up from the chair as he spoke. "I'll find some way to get word to your mother."

While Dad went into town to call a boardinghouse in Willows, California, Clayton, Sid, and I wandered around the lighthouse not doing much of anything. Whenever I sat down, Clayton was in my lap. About midmorning, Sid had had enough. He began to work frantically, attacking the lighthouse as if it were an obstacle to be overcome instead of our home. He polished the brightwork and rinsed the deck. He washed the kitchen floor with angry stabs of the mop, sloshing water into the corners and down the hallway. He did two loads of laundry in the gas-powered washing machine, stomping on the start pedal as if he was punishing the old machine.

While Sid's grief made him work, mine weighed me down with lethargy. I felt drained. My body was heavy and sluggish. Even walking was an enormous effort. I sat in the sitting room looking out the window at the sky and shoreline in the distance until Clayton slid off my lap and tugged at my arm.

"Let's go outside, Weezie."

We walked out the back door into the summer sunshine. The sun sparkled on the water as it moved silently past the lighthouse. We sat down with our legs dangling off the deck, our faces poking out between the fence railings. A seagull wheeled and dipped across the air in front of us. An occasional horn or engine backfire drifted to us from the Hudson shore. A motorboat chugged by us and its inhabitants raised their arms in greeting. Clayton and I waved back. It seemed impossible that people could be honking horns and riding in their pleasure boats today. Not with Rudy dead onshore and us full of grief here in the lighthouse.

Clayton and I came in from the deck and found Sid sitting at the kitchen table with a pile of clothes in front of him.

"Sid? You doing laundry?" I tried to sound like I was making a joke. Even though we both knew he was doing laundry to keep from screaming.

He looked up at me with such pain on his face I had to look away. "What do I do with Rudy's clothes?" he said softly.

"They belong upstairs in his dresser," I said. "You know where they go."

"But—" Sid began.

"In his dresser!" I repeated. I scooped up the clothes before Sid could say anything else and ran up the stairs.

Dad came back later that afternoon. We met him in the hall-way.

"Did you talk to her?" I asked. "Is she coming home?"

Dad shook his head. "She's not there anymore. She's moved on."

Sid looked up from sweeping the sitting-room rug. "She ought to be at her own son's funeral," said Sid. "It ain't right." His voice began to rise. "She ain't right in doing this!" He gave the rug a violent poke with the broom.

"Isn't right," I muttered, and then agreed. "It isn't right at all."

In the two days leading up to the funeral, Dad went into town several times to make arrangements. He often came back with a homemade casserole for dinner made by someone in town. Mrs. Bennett, a woman who lived by the river almost opposite the lighthouse, came out on the day before the funeral and cleaned the house for us and cooked supper. People sent out trays of cookies, cakes, and vegetables. One man brought a hen. We didn't have the heart to kill it, so it wandered around the lighthouse deck, clucking and pecking at the concrete. Clayton named her Mrs. Little.

"She's Chicken Little's mother," he said. It was the first time he had smiled since the accident.

Mrs. Little was willing to pay for her keep. The morning after she arrived, I found an egg in the coil of rope near the dock lad-der. I started leaving the vegetable peelings and coffee grounds in a pan on the deck for her to eat. We all tried not to open the doors suddenly when going out onto the deck so as not to star-tle Mrs. Little and send her squawking.

Finally Wednesday came. We all dressed in our best clothes and went into town to the Dutch Reformed Church of Hudson.

The Reverend van Ort delivered the eulogy. He said the Lord gives and the Lord takes away. He said those who fear the Lord are righteous. He didn't say much about Rudy. Nothing about Rudy's smile or the way he'd sit at the kitchen table doing his homework. Or about the valentine he made for Mrs. Kelchner and how he almost drowned running after it in the wind 'cause when he loved someone, he loved them one hundred percent. The reverend didn't say anything about Rudy's mattress on the floor or how much he missed Ma and how he'd always help Clayton get dressed in the morning, even when we were late for school. He didn't say anything about me having to walk to school alone now. Nothing about Clayton crying next to me on the sofa for the past three days, wishing his big brother would come home. Or about Sid scrubbing the metal stairs of the lighthouse tower until his knuckles bled because he couldn't cry for Rudy. And the reverend didn't say anything about Dad, being strong and quiet, keeping us fed, tucking us into bed at night and with one less child to say good night to. Missing the one with an ache so big he couldn't breathe, and loving the other three just as hard.

He didn't mention Ma, either. She wasn't there. We couldn't find her to tell her that her middle son had been killed in the punt with his hand on the tiller of a little three-horse-power Johnson outboard motor.

Chapter Thirty-two

LATER, BACK AT THE LIGHTHOUSE, Clayton and I stood outside on the deck. We were having a sudden spate of heat, and the June sunshine, relentless and hot, made my head ache. We squinted against the glare and the sparkle coming up off the river.

"I miss Rudy," said Clayton.

My throat hurt so bad I could hardly talk, but I made my trembling lips move. "Me, too."

"Weezie?"

"Yes, Clayton."

"Rudy didn't like the top bunk."

"I know, sweetie."

Clayton heaved a great sigh. "He's not going to like it under-ground like that."

I was crying now. Nothing I could do to prevent the tears from coming out of my eyes. I unpinned Clayton's handkerchief from his shirt and blew my nose. I took Clayton by the shoulders and knelt down in front of him.

"That's not Rudy there in the ground," I said.

Clayton shook his head, his own chin trembling. Tears pooled at the corners of his eyes but did not fall. *Why is he forced to be this strong at five?* I thought to myself. *Where is the fairness in that?*

"But, Weezie, I saw him in that box. The casket." He sniffled and wiped his nose with his hand. "They're going to cover it with dirt, and Rudy won't like that." He started to cry quietly. "He really won't."

I blinked against the tears in my own eyes and squeezed Clayton's shoulders. I noticed that one of the buttons on his shirt-front was loose. It dangled crookedly, the thread a thin umbilical cord passing through the buttonhole.

"Listen to me, Clayton," I began. "You need to really listen to me."

He nodded.

"It doesn't matter about the dirt." I touched the loose button. "Rudy doesn't care anymore."

"But why, Weezie? Why doesn't he care?"

"That's not Rudy in the casket." I wiped my nose again. "It's just the part of him that we can see. The real part—the Rudy part—the Rudy we loved . . ." My voice cracked and I had to swallow again before continuing. "The Rudy we loved, the one that made you laugh and helped you get dressed. That part of Rudy will never die."

Clayton just looked at me silently. I could almost see his mind trying to understand what I was saying.

"The body in the casket—Rudy's body—is empty now. It doesn't have Rudy in it anymore. Rudy's spirit has gone to another place. Do you understand?"

He shrugged and looked down at his shoes. "Where did the Rudy part go? Heaven?"

"I don't know." I looked through the deck fence at the Athens shoreline. Everything was green and bright. A woman, tiny as a doll, walked along the shore. A dog's tail trailed behind her, a brown plume bobbing amid the tall shoreline grass. "Some people think our spirit just disappears. Dissipates into nowhere. Some people think the invisible part of us goes to heaven and lives on forever." I stood up and turned to face the river. "Some people think we become part of everything else that's alive, like the grass and the flowers and even other people."

"What do you think, Weezie?"

I turned back to Clayton. "I think Rudy knows the answer." I straightened up and smoothed my dress at the knees. "And we're left here to keep wondering and hoping."

Clayton's lip began to tremble anew, and he squeezed his eyes shut against tears. "I wish he was still here."

"Me, too." I hugged him to me and waited for him to stop crying. After a while, he pulled away from me and wiped his eyes.

"Is Ma dead, too?" he asked.

I shook my head. "No, Clayton. She's not dead." A great blue heron slid silently by in the air above us, its long wings stretched out to each side to embrace the wind. "She's still wondering and hoping, just like us."

He was quiet for a while. We both looked down at the river rushing by below. Bits of vegetation, sticks, and an occasional log were carried past. I watched an empty tin can bob close to the foundation and bang up against a rock before being swept downstream, its tattered paper label spread out behind it like a rudder. It was a little round boat holding nothing but air and the memory of what was once inside it. Perhaps in its former life it had held beans or little white potatoes. Maybe creamed corn that children had wrinkled their noses over, or pickled beets, dark red and dripping with the taste of the earth. Now it was just an empty can, the useful stuff inside it chewed and swallowed by some unknown diner. The molecules of corn or beets or beans absorbed and remade new into the molecules of a living, breathing human being.

I watched the can until my eyes could no longer distinguish it from the sparkling gray water of the river, then took Clayton by the hand as we walked back inside the lighthouse.

Chapter Thirty-three

JULY PASSED INTO AUGUST. Dad had sent word of Rudy's death through Ma's lawyer, the one who had sent the divorce papers.

"Maybe he'll be able to find her," he said.

Clayton turned six on August 15. Dad got him a bamboo fishing rod with a spinning reel. Clayton practiced casting with a wooden bob on the end of the line.

"'Bout time you joined the ranks of the fishermen in the family," said Dad.

One day in early September, just before school was to start, Sid took Clayton down on the rocks at the base of the lighthouse to fish.

It was still summertime hot. I sat on the rocks with them and stared into the water. My feet, suspended just below the surface of the water, were magnified. I wiggled my toes and felt the water swirl and dance between them.

Out across the water a boat floated by, pushed by the wind. Trees along the opposite shore reached their leafy arms toward the sky. I could hear the river calling my name with its soft, familiar voice. The voice had traveled from high in the mountains, where the river begins as a single shining teardrop shed by the clouds. By the time it passed the lighthouse, this tear of the clouds had multiplied and merged into a wide, swollen torrent of water surging toward the sea.

Everything anyone has ever said or cried or wished floats by the lighthouse. When I listened carefully, I could hear the hopes and joys and sadnesses of a thousand generations all carried by the strong, relentless current of the river.

"I'm going into town, kids!" Dad called from the deck.

I got up and waved. "I'll come."

Dad and I went into town while Sid and Clayton stayed fishing. Dad wanted to get a couple of things at Shufelt's Market and pick up the mail. At the corner of Main Street and Hudson Avenue, we split up.

"You get the mail, Weezie, and meet me at the market," said Dad.

Main Street wasn't too busy on a Tuesday afternoon. I stopped and looked in the window of Libby's Department Store. There was a hat in the window—a little woolen beret. It was a burnt orange color: the color of poplar and sycamore leaves in October. Thirty-five cents. Dad had already bought me two new dresses for school. I knew he didn't have extra money for something as unnecessary as a hat. It sure would be nice to have, though. I felt the top of my head, remembering the straw cloche and how it had felt to wear it. I looked at the little beret awhile longer, then started up the sidewalk to the post office. A few cars were parked in front of Tomlinson's Hardware. I waved at Mr. Tomlinson through the window as I walked by.

There was one car parked in front of the post office. I pushed the door open and walked inside.

Mrs. Baskin, the postmistress, was not a tall woman. She was standing behind the counter, and I could just see the top of her head. She was looking down at something below the level of the counter. She glanced up at me as the door shut, but didn't stop what she had been doing. I stood for several seconds at the counter before she looked up at me.

"Hello, Miss Bloom," she said.

"Hello, Mrs. Baskin. Anything for us today?" I smiled. One of the ongoing bets between us kids was to see if one of us could get Mrs. Baskin to crack a smile. So far, none of us had been successful.

Mrs. Baskin went to a wall of cubbyholes to the left of the counter. She reached into one near the bottom and pulled out a handful of envelopes. Then she bent down and lifted something from the floor. It was a small box wrapped in brown paper and tied with string.

"Quite a bundle there," she said, and handed me the mail over the counter. "Looks like you got something from Arkansas."

My heart lurched in my chest. I quickly put the envelopes on top of the box so that I couldn't read the address. "Thank you."

"Any news from your mother?" asked Mrs. Baskin.

I shook my head. "No, ma'am."

Mrs. Baskin shook her head. "It's a shame, you poor things." She clucked her tongue. "Disgrace."

I turned and hurried out of the post office. I walked slowly, staring at the ground. I tried not to think about the package pressing against my waist.

The Queen Anne's lace and cornflowers along the sidewalk called out in blue and white voices. *Heard anything from your mother?* they asked. The bees hummed and sang on their endless circuit between flower and hive. *Don't answer, don't answer,* whispered the blue cornflowers. My hipbone bumped against the bottom of the package each time I took a step. I could feel the heat of the sidewalk seeping up through my shoes.

I met Dad coming out of Shufelt's Market with two bags of groceries clutched against his sides.

"We got a package, Dad," I said. "From Arkansas." I was as out of breath as if I had been running.

"That so?" he asked.

I nodded and lifted the envelopes from the top of the box. It was about the size of a shoebox. Dad cocked his head to better read the address on top. "Sid, Louise, and Clayton Bloom," he said. "No return address."

"Arkansas postmark," I said.

"Guess you're right," said Dad. "You'll have to wait till we get back to the lighthouse. It's got your brothers' names on it, too."

We started back toward the river. I looked at the top of the box again. "She knows about Rudy," I said.

"Guess so," said Dad. He squinted at the Queen Anne's lace beside the road. "Guess so."

Chapter Thirty-four

CLAYTON GRABBED FOR THE BOX. "Let me open it!" he said.

"I'm the oldest," said Sid. He reached out and slipped the box from under my arm. We were upstairs in the hallway.

"I carried it from the post office!" I whirled around and lunged at the box. Sid, smiling, held it above his head.

"Sorry, too short."

"No fair!" squeaked Clayton. He bobbed up and down beside me, his little hands flapping in front of Sid's face as he reached for the box.

"Sid, let me have that!"

"Sid, let me have that," mimicked Sid. "No fair."

"I want to open it!" screamed Clayton. Sid blinked and lowered the package.

"All right, for pity's sake," he said. He gave the package to Clayton, who snatched it out of his hands. "I don't care about a lousy package from Arkansas, anyhow."

Clayton walked down the hall to his room and sat on the lower bunk. Rudy's mattress was still on the floor, and Sid and I sat down on it.

"Okay, Clayton," I sighed. "Let's see what's in there."

Clayton tore off the string and the brown paper wrapping.

Inside the box was mostly newspaper. Clayton carefully removed each crumpled piece and handed it to me. Finally he held up a small cloth bag with a drawstring top.

"What is it?" asked Sid.

I wanted to grab the bag from Clayton, but I kept my hands in my lap around the balls of crumpled paper.

Sid made a halfhearted swipe at the bag. "Open the thing, Clayton, or I'll do it."

Clayton clutched the bag to him, then undid the string at the top and worked the bag open. He dumped the contents into his hand. "It's rocks!"

"Rocks?" I moved to the bed beside Clayton. There were half a dozen small, smoky crystals resting in the palm of Clayton's hand.

Sid leaned forward and picked one up with his finger and thumb.

I looked in the bottom of the box and lifted out an envelope. "There's a letter."

"Jesus," said Sid. "Just what we need. A letter."

"Stop swearing!" said Clayton. He wiped his nose with the back of his free hand.

"Didn't know it bothered you," said Sid. He lay back on the mattress and held the rock above his face. "Might as well read it, Louise."

Clayton snuffled again but didn't say anything.

I lifted the flap on the envelope and pulled out a single sheet of folded paper. Clayton leaned against me, and Sid stared at the rock rolling between his finger and thumb as I began to read.

The letter wasn't long. I remember hearing my voice echo

around the little room as I read. Sid and Clayton were perfectly quiet, listening to every word as it traveled from the page to my lips and out across the air.

Ma wrote that she missed us and wanted to see us. Her heart ached for Rudy, and children, can you forgive me for leaving? She wrote someday maybe we'd understand. She said Arkansas was beautiful, more beautiful than what she was used to after living in New York for so long. She said she used to stand on the deck looking out from the lighthouse and see nothing but trees and that ugly, constant river, and now she was seeing so much more. She said enjoy the diamonds, though they are only industrial diamonds. I dug them myself in a mine underground. And God watch over Rudy. She wrote that she missed us and maybe next spring she'd be in upstate New York. But don't get your hopes up, children, I'm not sure where I'll be. She said she remained our loving mother.

And that was all she wrote.

If you were coming in the Fall,
I'd brush the Summer by
With half a smile, and half a spurn,
As Housewives do a fly.
—EMILY DICKINSON

Chapter Thirty-five

SCHOOL STARTED THE DAY AFTER LABOR DAY. My freshman year. At breakfast, Clayton was chattering pretty much nonstop.

"I've got three pencils," he said. "Is that enough?" He lifted a dripping spoonful of Ralston flakes toward his mouth with his right hand and brandished the pencils, their dark, sharp points toward me, in his left.

"It's enough to start with," I said.

"Crayons, too!" said Clayton. "I like green the best. What's your favorite color, Sid?"

"Green's pretty good," said Sid as he crossed the kitchen toward the pantry.

"Yup. I like green. What time is lunch?" continued Clayton. "Did you put a cookie in my lunch, Weezie?"

"Yes, Clayton. Now finish your breakfast. We need to get moving."

Clayton wiped his nose on his napkin and took another spoonful of cereal. He had a clean handkerchief pinned to his shirt and another one in his back pocket.

"Don't know what I'm going to do around here without my Right-Hand Man," said Dad. He rubbed the top of Clayton's head so that his hair stood up on end.

"I can help you when I get home from school," said Clayton, looking concerned.

Dad nodded and smiled. "Guess I can manage until then."

I folded down the waxed-paper bag inside the cereal box and took it to the pantry. Somebody had torn off one of the flaps from the top of the box. I tried to close the box and gave up.

Sid was in the pantry opening a can of baking powder.

"You baking this morning?"

He rolled his eyes at me and turned the can upside down. Nothing came out, and he lifted the can over this head and peered inside. He stuck a finger in and came out with a wad of crumpled strips of thin cardboard.

"What—" I said, and stopped. The box top from the Ralston flakes was clutched in his other hand.

"Rudy's box tops," I said.

Sid nodded and put the cover back on the empty baking-powder can. "I think there's enough now."

"What are you going to get?"

"Not for me," said Sid. "For Rudy." He looked at me and shrugged. "He wanted the Tom Mix stuff." I saw two spots of color on his cheeks and realized he was embarrassed.

"That's nice of you, Sid. I know Rudy would be real happy about that."

He cleared his throat and looked at the box tops in his hand.

"Let's go!" said Clayton. His head appeared around the corner of the pantry. He was grinning and bobbing up and down. "I want to go!"

I took an envelope from the sideboard as we left the lighthouse and handed it to Sid as we stepped off on the Hudson shore.

"I'll see you this afternoon," Dad said as Sid pushed the punt back into the current.

We started up toward the railroad tracks.

"Doesn't seem right without Rudy," said Sid.

"I know," I said. "It isn't."

Clayton tugged at my sleeve. "You're coming inside with me, right, Weezie?"

I nodded.

"We'll both come in," said Sid. He cuffed Clayton on the shoulder. "Don't worry, you're going to be the smartest kid in first grade."

We headed across the railroad tracks toward town, Clayton's shoes kicking up the pebbles along the rail bed and Sid's heavy foot treads beating an uneven rhythm against the ground beneath us.

I stopped to look back and saw Dad in the punt pulling slowly toward the lighthouse. I wondered if he felt lonely in a small boat on such a big river. It was the very bigness of the river that always made me feel safe, somehow. Like I was being carried in the palm of a great, swaying hand. I turned back toward town. Sid and Clayton were already past the train station. "Clayton! Sid!" I called. "Wait!"

They both turned and watched as I hurried to join them. The empty column of air that should have been Rudy walked silently beside us all the way to school.

Chapter Thirty-six

THE TOM MIX JUNIOR DEPUTY KIT (*Exciting! Authentic!*) was delivered the first week of October. The leaves were in their full autumn color and the sky was that clear, light blue that only happens in the fall.

Sid, Clayton, and I walked to the cemetery after school the day after the deputy stuff arrived. The cemetery is on a hill on the south edge of town that overlooks the river. It is a place I know that Rudy would have liked. He never saw it when he was alive. We didn't have a reason to come up here. But there's a real pretty view of the Presbyterian church with its tall spire and of the Mesicks' dairy farm below it. If you stand on your tiptoes at the top of the hill you can see the lighthouse tower just peeking over the tops of the trees by the river.

The three of us stood quietly in front of Rudy's grave.

Sid reached into his backpack.

"Here," he said, handing me a badge made of pressed tin. He handed Clayton a silver six-shooter. Sid held what looked like a pair of tin spurs. Clayton stepped forward and put the six-shooter on top of the headstone.

"That's for you, Rudy," he said. "Hope you like it."

I don't know how long we stood there with the wind tilting the leaves on their stems and the sleepy autumn crickets making their final chirps in the grass. Our shadows slowly crept outward from our feet and the leaves drifted down, tipping and spiraling on the air like falling dancers against the sky.

Later, back at the lighthouse, I stood outside the lantern room looking out from the tower railing. That's where I'm standing now.

The river spreads out from me in both directions, lined on each side with rolling blankets of gold, orange, and red. The Iroquois who have lived here since long before there was a lighthouse think that the autumn colors come from the blood and fat of a great bear in the sky killed by three brothers long, long ago. At night, they say, you can still see the brothers chasing that bear if you look at the stars. I'm sure it's true. There are lots of things you can see in the stars if you look carefully enough.

I like to think of the leaves as summer's way of going out with one final, glorious hurrah. The colors call to us like travelers waving bright handkerchiefs as they stand along a boat rail ready for some long journey. *See you next year!* they shout. *Don't forget us! Take care!* We stand on the pier, wistfully returning their waves with our own empty hands, watching the boat glide away as we stay motionless on shore. *Bon voyage,* we whisper. *Bon voyage.*

The leaves along the Hudson are really beautiful this year. The river is crowded during the day with people who have come from all over the United States to see them. People come from as far away as Arkansas and California to see the same ordinary sycamore, oak, and hickory leaves I'm looking at right now. These tourists will probably send postcards to their people back home and tell them how lovely it all is. *Magnificent and breathtaking,* they'll write. *Simply gorgeous.* They'll be telling the truth. It is lovely.

These visitors can see the beauty in the view from the lighthouse. I wish Ma could. But I know there is no sense wishing for things that just can't be. The sun is beginning to set now, spreading brilliant pink and orange across the low clouds on the horizon. If you saw it in a painting, you would say the artist made it up. Nothing could be that pink. The dark surface of the river is a mirror reflecting the colors above and below.

I hear the clank and scrape of someone climbing the spiral staircase to the lantern room.

"Hello, Louise," says Dad. "What're you up to?"

I nod toward the pink horizon and the autumn leaves. "Watching the sunset."

Dad stands beside me and I hear his breath come out in a sigh. "Awful pretty, isn't it?"

"Yes," I say. "It truly is."

"I've got something for you," says Dad. He holds a tissue-wrapped something out to me.

Inside the tissue is the burnt orange beret from Libby's Department Store window. A warm glow starts in my stomach and moves up to my face in a smile.

"How did you know?"

Dad shrugs. "You've always liked the fall leaves. The color made me think of you."

"Thanks, Dad." I hug him for a long time.

"You're welcome," he says.

I put the hat on. The beret sits on top of my head instead of down around my eyebrows like the old straw cloche. The beret is not a hat to hide in. This new hat feels snug and jaunty and completely mine. It is a hat to be happy in.

"I joined the high school Glee Club today," I say.

"Good for you, Weezie," says Dad. "You've always loved to sing."

Dad goes back down the stairs, and I am alone again. Under the warm pink glow of the fading sunset, I see the river and the shoreline, then the town, and the trees rising up above the town. Farther still, beyond the trees and the farm fields, I can see the majestic lines of the Catskill Mountains rising up out of the darkening forest.

From the lighthouse, I can see the hill where Rudy is buried. And if I stand on tiptoe, I can almost see his grave with the Tom Mix Deputy Kit resting on top.

As I stand here looking out from the railing, something magical happens: the river sends me a song. It is faint at first, like a distant whisper, and I can't quite make out the words. It grows louder, and as the melody fills my head, suddenly the words gallop and somersault up from my throat and out over my tongue. I lift my face toward the setting sun and sing to the river, to the sky, and to the glorious, burning leaves.

I'm not waiting for Ma anymore. I know I'll see her again someday, if not next spring then perhaps the one after that, and that is enough for now. Let Ma go searching for views from other houses across other tree lines and distant hills.

The view from the lighthouse suits me just fine.

From the building of the first lighthouse at Stony Point in 1826, until the present day, lighthouses have played an important part in the history of the Hudson River. Over the years, there have been as many as fourteen lighthouses and numerous post lights up and down the river. Today only seven lighthouses remain.

Lighthouse keepers employed by the United States Lighthouse Service lived in the lighthouses and tended the lights. They had many jobs: cleaning the giant glass lens that magnified and housed the light, polishing the brass fittings and railings, repairing and maintaining the lighthouse and boats, keeping careful records of weather and river conditions, even rescuing people from the river. Their most important job was to "never let the light go out" so that ships could travel up and down the river safely, between the port in New York City and the point near Troy, New York, where the Hudson River meets the Erie and Champlain Canals.

The Hudson-Athens Lighthouse (originally called the Hudson City Lighthouse), where this story takes place, is now the northernmost lighthouse on the river. It was built in 1874 between the shores of Hudson City, New York, and Athens, New York, to guide ships around a shallow part of the river called the Middle Ground Flats.

Hudson, where Weezie and her brothers go to school and get

the mail, is a real town. There actually was a Fourth Street School and a new high school on Harry Howard Avenue in the 1930s. Some other places exist only in this book: Shufelt's Market and Tomlinson's Hardware store, for example. If you visit the city of Hudson, you can go to the river and look out across the water, and you will see the lighthouse with its light tower and iron deck railing; and beyond that, the town of Athens on the western shore.

The kerosene light in the Hudson City Lighthouse was first lit on November 14, 1874. Lighthouse keepers lived in the lighthouse and tended the lamp until November 10, 1949, when the light was automated. Today, the Hudson-Athens Lighthouse continues to guide ships around the Middle Ground Flats with a solar-powered beacon.

The last keeper to actually reside in the lighthouse was Emil Brunner, who lived there with his family in the 1930s. This story isn't about the Brunners, but some of the things in Weezie's story—like the game of Telephone and walking to school across the ice—come from accounts by Emily Brunner about her time spent living in the lighthouse with four younger brothers.

A few years after Mr. Brunner left, the lighthouse was automated and boarded up for almost thirty years. The Hudson-Athens Lighthouse Preservation Society was formed in 1982. Society volunteers work to repair and restore the structure and to educate people about the important role that this and other lighthouses played in the history of the Hudson River. A museum is being planned, and the Society gives tours of the lighthouse during the summer and fall.

You can see pictures of Emily and her brothers as children and learn more about what it was like to live in the lighthouse by contacting the Preservation Society (P.O. Box 145, Athens, New

York 12015; website: http://hometown.aol.com.thelightkeeper/ Hudson-AthensLighthouse.html). Information about the Hudson-Athens Lighthouse can also be found on the website of the Hudson River Lighthouse Coalition (www.hudsonlights.com).